I0642764

NUCLEAR GHOSTS

Haunted Wastelands Series
BOOK 2

IAN FORTEY
AND
RON RIPLEY

EDITED BY ANNE LAO
AND DAWN KLEMISH

ISBN: 979-8-89476-291-3
Copyright © 2025 by ScareStreet.com

All rights reserved. This book or any portion thereof may not be reproduced or used in any manner whatsoever without written permission from the publisher except for the use of brief quotations in a book review.

This is a work of fiction. Any resemblance to actual persons, living or dead, or actual events is purely coincidental.

Enter the Realm of Terror...

We'd like to take a moment to thank you for your support and invite you to join our VIP newsletter.

Dive deeper into the darkness with exclusive offers, early access to new releases, and bone-chilling deals when you sign up at www.ScareStreet.com.

Let the nightmares begin…

See you in the shadows,
Scare Street

PROLOGUE

A breeze in the Mojave sounded like a distant waterfall. When the wind kicked up and there was so much open space, it became a roar. It rose and fell like waves, and the faint pattering of sand against your clothing and flesh was the only variation you'd hear, like a bit of texture added to the smoothness of nature's aggression.

Harland Supp turned away from the wind. The night was cold again, a contrast from the day's heat, but dry. The mixture of dry air and dust stung his eyes, and he found that some nights left the corners of his mouth and nostrils caked with little balls of mud from it.

He and Ryne McKendry had guarded Bunker 7 for nearly three months. A full twelve-hour shift every night, in the dark, and in the middle of nowhere.

The two men barely spoke for the first two nights. They had been ordered not to. Harland didn't know McKendry, so the two had no reason to speak about anything. On the third night, Harland accidentally dropped his thermos of coffee in the sand and cursed much louder than was necessary. It didn't matter: No one else was around for miles.

McKendry offered Harland a Pepsi. It wasn't coffee, but he always brought three with him, and Harland was glad to have something. They both had water, but it was nice to cut the monotony with some flavor. It was impossible to avoid a mouthful of dust by the end of the shift, and the taste was not desirable.

From that day on, the two engaged in normal workplace small talk and then friendlier banter. It was clear that no one was monitoring them or checking their work. There were no functional cameras outside of the bunker, and their guard station was little more than a glorified box with a toilet and a sink inside.

Neither knew why they were guarding the bunker, what was in it, or who owned it. The Nevada National Security Site was an alphabet soup of jurisdiction. The Army covered some spots and the Air Force others, not to mention the U.S. Geological Survey, the Department of Energy, the Atomic Energy Commission, and probably a handful of others. Not that it mattered. A job was a job.

They were on a six-month contract, and it was a hell of a thing to work twelve hours a day for six months straight, but the money was absurd. He, so far, had made more standing in the desert talking with McKendry than he had in two full years at the best job he'd ever had previously. He was not complaining at all.

Harland and McKendry were armed. Harland had never had to kill anyone, but he had been fired upon and returned fire. He'd served two tours in Vietnam. He would not hesitate to use a weapon if it came to that. But in three months, they hadn't even seen a coyote, let alone a human. They didn't even get lizards.

McKendry was cagey about his military history. He hadn't served in Vietnam, but he said he had been out of the country until seventy-three. He had been back less than a year when he got the job guarding Bunker 7.

For three months, nothing at all had happened at the bunker, and then, that morning, they had been informed that a VIP would arrive during their shift. All they had to do was make sure he got safely into and out of the bunker.

"Like a doorman?" McKendry reviewed the orders on site.

Each of them had the paperwork hand-delivered to their homes by a nameless man in a suit that evening before their shifts started.

"We're doormen," Harland agreed, his back still to the wind.

McKendry chuckled and shrugged.

"What do you think is going on down in there?"

"Nuclear stuff. Spy stuff. Hell, I don't know," Harland replied.

He'd thought of it before. They did all kinds of nuclear tests out in the desert, and he'd heard they had been doing them since the 1950s. They had to keep up with stuff so the Soviets wouldn't get ahead. That made sense.

"Never seen any tracks in or out of here, is all," McKendry said. "No one comes here but us."

"Yeah."

Harland had noticed that as well. There was no day shift that they relieved, nor did any take over for them in the morning when they left their posts. It was the two of them and no one else.

It was closing in on three in the morning when a new sound cut through the moaning of the wind in the dark desert. Harland and McKendry were alert and ready for it as a pair of headlights appeared on the horizon.

The men waited, rifles at the ready, as an Army Jeep approached, hitting every bump and stone in the desert along the way as it approached the bunker.

The Jeep slowed to a stop just a few yards from the men. The driver was alone and got out slowly, using the frame of the vehicle to support himself. He wore a polo shirt and khaki pants, no sign that he was military or government. His hair was cropped short, but Harland didn't think he was in the service based on the way he carried himself.

The stranger was pale and had deep bags under his eyes like he hadn't slept in days. "Is the door unlocked?" the man asked. He sounded out of breath and gruff.

"No," McKendry answered. "We don't have access."

The man at the Jeep sighed loudly, almost forcing out a laugh, and shook his head. He reached back into the Jeep and pulled out what looked like a jewelry box or something used for keepsakes. Dark wood, bigger than a shoebox, and heavy, judging from the way the man held it.

He grunted, holding it at chest level and walking toward the two guards. The strain of carrying the box seemed to hit the man immediately, and Harland saw he was tensing, holding his breath as his face flushed red in the glow of the Jeep's headlights.

"You need a hand?" Harland was unsure if the man was supposed to be referred to as "sir".

"No," the man snapped breathily. "No one touches it. Just get the door."

"The door's locked." McKendry gestured with his thumb to the bunker. "We've never been inside."

McKendry approached the bunker door. Bunker 7 was little more than a slanted stone wall that vanished into the sand, with a red, steel door in the center of it. It was slightly larger than their guard station. The door must have led to a set of stairs because there was no room for anything inside the tiny structure aboveground, but that was all Harland or his partner knew.

McKendry grabbed the handle on the door and pushed it down. The mechanism inside crunched and squealed, and the door pulled open in his grip. He looked at Harland, stunned by the revelation, and Harland shrugged.

The man with the box stumbled a couple of paces from the Jeep and stopped, half-crouched and hugging the box like it was the most precious thing he owned.

"Sir," Harland said, stepping toward him.

"Back up!" the man demanded.

He breathed heavily, straining even more now, and straightened. A drop of blood hung from the man's right nostril, dangling precariously until he took another unsteady step, and then it fell onto the sand. Another followed, and then another, and soon, a full nosebleed ran openly from both nostrils.

"Hey, pal, your nose is running like a tap." McKendry grimaced slightly.

The man looked confused and then looked down. Blood had splattered against his hands and the box he clutched. As Harland watched, the blood on the box dried out, darkening and sticking to the wooden surface.

"Doesn't matter." The man leaned his head awkwardly to the right so he could wipe his nose on his shoulder. "Let's go. Quickly."

Harland didn't want to get any closer to the man, but he walked at his side like an official escort. The man groaned and wobbled suddenly, falling to his knees as he lost his grip on the box. It tumbled from his hands, and he nearly went face-first into the sand, catching himself on one shaky arm at the last moment.

"Sir, you need medical attention," Harland said.

He had no idea what was wrong with the man and hoped it wasn't contagious.

"I'm fine." The man struggled to get the words out and coughed hoarsely. His body shuddered and blood splattered his hand from the effort.

"I—"

He tried to speak several times, to stand or even move, but the coughing took hold. Harland had no idea what to do. He knew basic field medicine, but that was for injuries. He could handle cuts, breaks, and even a bullet wound in a pinch. Whatever the man was dealing with was beyond his knowledge.

"Call it in," Harland said to McKendry.

They had one walkie-talkie between them that neither had ever used. It was strictly for emergencies, and they had been warned to only use it in a life-or-death situation. Harland assumed this was such a situation.

"Base, this is Bunker 7. We have a medical emergency," McKendry said into the walkie. He removed his finger from the button, and there was no reply, not even static.

5

"Base?" he said again, tweaking the volume. Still nothing.

McKendry cycled through the channels as Harland got the man on the ground to lay on his side.

"This thing's got no signal," McKendry said.

"The box," the man finally said forcefully, struggling against Harland. "Give... me..."

"The box can wait—" Harland began, leaning over to pick it up. He grabbed the sides of it and lifted. It was heavier than he expected, but it was also upside-down. The lid popped open, and a human skull rolled out into the sand.

The stranger was still trying to stand when McKendry dropped the walkie.

"Harland," he said softly.

Harland watched as the skull began to glow. The light was soft at first but grew steadily brighter.

The stranger flopped onto his back, his eyes wide with terror as the light bathed them all, now as bright as a bulb.

"Run!" he barked, blood and spit streaming from his lips. "Run, goddamn you!"

Harland winced and dropped the box, lifting his arm to shield himself from the ever-brightening light. It burned his eyes, and he could barely see as he turned away to find some relief.

McKendry cried out in pain, and an instant later, Harland felt a searing burn along the bare flesh of his arm and the back of his neck. He shrunk away from it to conceal himself, but soon, it was across his body, even beneath his flesh.

The stranger was screaming. McKendry's howl was like an animal, and Harland ran. He stumbled, his boots melting from his feet and flames licking along his back as his clothing ignited. He felt his flesh cracking and burning down to the muscle.

He fell to the ground in agony, unable to do anything but scream into the dry, dusty Mojave as his flesh and muscle and finally bone was scorched to nothing.

Chapter 1
Beyond Yucca Flat

Shane was relieved to leave Las Vegas behind him for the last time. The drive northwest out of the city through the desert was devoid of sights beyond rocks, sand, and cacti.

Ventura rode shotgun in Shane's car and after about half an hour, the FBI agent had run out of things to say. Even though he had contributed greatly to solving the murders of several tourists in the Mojave Desert, he was still on forced vacation from the bureau. It weighed heavily on him that he had not found himself back in the bureau's good graces.

The Las Vegas branch of the FBI had thanked him for his assistance, but no one offered to bring him back to the East Coast and get him back on active duty. His involvement in the Las Vegas case, as well as the capture of Bennett Ross, had been considered little more than a civilian assist. They had regarded Shane's involvement the same way.

Putting a stop to the ghost that had committed the murders and ending Bennett—who had sold stolen and, in some cases radioactive, haunted items—had been Shane and Ventura's goal. But in doing so, they'd opened a new can of worms that led them beyond the old nuclear test sites in Nevada.

Ross had found a source of ghosts whose items had been irradiated. Not only were the ghosts dangerous, but their items could potentially kill as well. Shane wanted to find out where they had come from, and so did Ventura. But this was not something the FBI could help with. A murderer and a smuggler, they understood. Ghosts were not their purview.

The ghosts had come from somewhere in the old nuclear test

grounds, but there was a lot of desert to cover, and no one would help them get access. Ventura had already tried an Air Force contact and was shot down almost immediately. That meant Shane would have to take the lead on doing things a bit less legally. Ventura, for his part, seemed willing to go along with some minor trespassing and breaking and entering. Shane didn't ask so the other man didn't have to answer.

Their destination was a town called Benton, located west of Yucca Flat. Wedged between the national security site on one side and Death Valley on the other, it was almost literally the middle of nowhere.

Benton had a population of less than one hundred people. It was mostly a tourist stop for people on their way to somewhere better who hoped to get a look at where the bombs were tested half a century earlier. The town's main feature was a diner with a disarmed nuclear bomb in the parking lot. People took pictures with it. The diner was called the Fission Chips Diner. It was morbidly clever.

Next to the diner was the Benton Inn, which was a nice name for a motel that looked like a bomb would have improved it. Shane had seen some rough motels before, but the Benton Inn was almost absurd in its disrepair.

The sign out front was missing the "B", but the sun had bleached the wall enough that the outline was still visible. The siding was falling away in more than one place, and weeds grew through the cracks in the walkway in front of the rooms to the point that some of the cement slabs pushed up at thirty-degree angles.

"This place looks like it was built in the fifties," Ventura said as they pulled in. "Is it even still in business?"

Shane gestured to the office where, through the curtainless windows, they saw a man sitting at a desk.

There were no cars in the lot. Shane pulled in next to the office and looked across the available rooms. There were eight in total, stretched down the length of the longhouse-style building. One had no windows, just boards, and only four rooms had numbers still attached to the doors.

They entered the office together, trading the scorching Nevada sun for a forty-watt bulb in an office with no air circulation that smelled like cured meat and mildew. It was at least five degrees hotter than outside.

"You got any vacancies?" Shane asked.

The man at the counter wore an undershirt and read an old Mack Bolan paperback. He looked like he was in his seventies and wore glasses as thick as Coke bottles.

"You bet." He didn't look at Shane until he'd finished the page he was on. He dog-eared the corner of the paper and closed the book, eyeing Shane and Ventura.

"One or two?" the man asked.

Shane glanced at Ventura.

"He snores. We need two," he said.

"One and two for ya." The old man slapped two key chains down on the desk. "AC don't work, but they got fans. Ice machine don't work. Cable don't work. Shower in two ain't the hottest but give it about five minutes. Sixty per night. Each."

"All that for sixty bucks, wow." Ventura pulled out a credit card before Shane could get his wallet. "We're staying two days."

"Times are tough," the old man said.

"I see. You know about any tours or anything out into the desert? Yucca Flat or any of the old military stuff?" Ventura asked.

The old man ran the credit card and gave Ventura a receipt along with both keys.

"No tours. Place is radioactive; you don't want to go out there. Got that alien town on the other side, Rachel, but you're a couple hundred miles west if that's what you want."

"No Area 51 stuff," Ventura said. "Just interested in where they tested the bombs."

"You can head to Burly Hill a few miles east. Got a good camera lens, you can get some photos of the desert, but it's all behind the fence."

"So they don't let people in anywhere?" Shane asked.

"To the radioactive, secure government site that's hundreds of miles from the nearest town, which you're currently in? No sir, they don't."

Shane grunted and took his key.

"Great. How's the coffee in the diner?"

"Wet," the old man replied. "Checkout's at noon."

A moment of silence marked the end of their conversation, and the man returned to Mack Bolan.

Ventura shrugged as Shane turned and walked back outside. They walked together down the uneven footpath to their rooms, which were in descending order from the office.

"I call One," Ventura said, swapping keys with Shane. "You get the busted shower."

"After I let you pay? Harsh, Agent Ventura." Shane opened the door to his room.

It was everything he expected it to be and less. The smell was not that bad, thanks to an air freshener that left it smelling vaguely like a hospital. But it was small and spartan and very hot. He found a desk fan on a nightstand and turned it on, listening to it squeal as the blades rotated, and left it running. Maybe by nightfall, the room would be tolerable.

Shane washed up quickly, frowning at the rust-stained tub and shower, and then headed back out to get Ventura. The agent was still in his room, so Shane knocked and waited for a reply.

"You want to trade rooms?" Ventura opened the door. His room had a burn mark in the carpet and smelled like melted plastic.

"Nah. Let's get some food," Shane suggested.

They left their bags in the car and walked from the motel across a second dirt parking lot to Fission Chips. Unlike the motel, the diner at least had some customers and seemed like it might be a popular spot for townspeople. The place was half-full in the middle of the day.

Like the motel, the diner appeared to be a relic from the fifties, complete with an L-shaped counter with barstools in the center that blocked off the kitchen.

A waitress in a skirt and a little paper hat told them to sit wherever they liked. There was a hum of conversation and some old rock-and-roll music playing from a jukebox at the far side of the dining area near the restrooms.

Shane chose a booth near the front window that looked out on the parking lot and the highway they'd come in on. The locals, or maybe tourists, ignored them as they took a seat.

The server took their orders quickly, despite how busy the place was, and they had coffee in less than five minutes along with some ice water. Ventura took his time with the menu, mulling over a burger or a club sandwich while Shane ordered a sandwich.

"We need a starting point. Ross' guys had to have an in, someplace easy to find, easy to come and go from without raising too many alarms even if someone was helping them," Shane said after the waitress left.

"Maybe an access road or something," Ventura mused. "But it has to lead somewhere, right?"

"I think none of this is on the books," Shane said. "Suppose there were people killed in these tests, intentionally or even by accident. Ross and his guys would be doing someone a favor in getting rid of the evidence."

"But it's decades later," Ventura said. "Who could possibly be held accountable for it now? If someone found the bodies, it'd be easy enough to say they were trespassing, and their deaths were a tragic accident because of tests conducted by officials who are all also long dead."

"The dead aren't quite that old." The man stood at the end of the table next to their booth.

Shane had not seen or heard him approach. Judging by Ventura's reaction to the sudden statement, neither had he.

As Ventura tensed, his hand creeping toward the weapon holstered under his jacket, Shane sighed audibly as he looked up at Thomas Coulson.

"Jesus," Shane muttered.

"Not quite, but we both came back from the dead, so I'll allow it," Coulson said.

He pushed his way into the booth, forcing Shane to shift over to allow him room. He wore the same pale-colored duster that he'd had on when Shane last saw him, not that he expected the man to have changed his clothes. Coulson wasn't really alive, so any changes in his appearance were arbitrary.

Ventura's eyes darted from Coulson to Shane and back.

"Thomas Coulson." The man extended a hand across the table. Ventura took it after a brief hesitation.

"Xander Ventura. I take it you two know each other."

"Shane and me? Oh God, we go way back. We once blew up a mountain with a nuclear bomb. Seems only appropriate we're here now. Nukes are our thing."

Shane took a drink from his coffee and shrugged after seeing the confused look on Ventura's face.

Coulson was not lying. They had once used a nuclear weapon in a mountain to put an end to the Endless Night. Coulson had left out some important details, not the least of which was that he was a ghost who could fool the living into thinking he was one of them.

When Thomas Coulson was alive, he'd been a man of singular talent. He could read minds and even move things with his own, an honest-to-goodness psychic and telekinetic. In death, he'd used those same powers to bind his spirit to the physical world. He had no haunted item, he simply existed wherever and whenever he wanted like any living man. People could see him, talk to him, and even touch him.

Coulson had all the strengths of a ghost but few, if any, of their weaknesses. Shane had fought him once when they were at odds after their first meeting, and while the ghost had struggled with him, Shane had struggled more. He could not fight Coulson like he fought other spirits. Coulson was too powerful.

Fortunately for Shane, their confrontation was short-lived, and they eventually worked together to save Carl and Coulson's girlfriend Jillian from the Endless Night.

They had parted on good enough terms, but Shane didn't fully trust Thomas Coulson. He had once broken into the house on Berkley Street and left with Carl's remains. Shane didn't trust the power the man wielded, and he knew, if forced, Coulson would do whatever he thought was right regardless of whether Shane agreed. And Shane wasn't sure he could stop him.

"Coulson's dead." Shane finished his coffee. "I'm sure he's here to make our lives more difficult."

"Not at all," the ghost said. "I'm here to make my life more difficult and bring you along for the ride."

CHAPTER 2
DEAD MAN'S TALES

"I don't understand," Ventura said.

The waitress had brought their food, and his hamburger sat half-eaten on his plate, forgotten as he was caught up in the enigma of the ghost. He watched Coulson like the not-man was a zoo animal, and Shane could tell Ventura wanted to reach out and touch him. He imagined Coulson, given what his abilities were, knew it, too.

"I had an odd death." Coulson shrugged.

Shane was not familiar with the details of Coulson's passing, and he had accepted that he probably didn't want to know them. Coulson and his partner Jillian had done some weird work in the past, fighting ghosts and demons with their abilities. They were part of a group that used its psychic abilities to combat spirits and other dark forces. Shane had once heard that Coulson had died literally saving the world, whatever that meant.

"But you're here," Ventura said. "Everyone can see you."

There was an intangible quality to a living human form that differed from that of a spirit. It was hard to articulate, but Shane knew a ghost when he saw one. It was like looking at photorealistic art that didn't quite get something right. No matter how much they looked like their former, living selves, ghosts always had that off quality. All except Thomas Coulson.

Coulson looked real. He smelled real, with whiffs of tobacco smoke, leather, or sweat following him. His clothing made a sound as it stretched and distressed. His shoes squeaked on floors. The booth depressed under his weight. Everything about him was perfectly alive.

The waitress had asked if Coulson wanted to order something. He had requested a cup of coffee though he had not touched it since it had arrived. It was just for show. Shane wondered how he planned to pay for it.

"What do you know about the radioactive ghosts?" Shane didn't want to waste time with the dozens of questions he knew Ventura would ask.

The agent looked at Shane unsurely. If it had been anyone else, Shane wouldn't have mentioned it, but he knew the only reason Coulson was there was because he already knew what was happening. That was how Coulson worked.

"Doomtown," the ghost answered. "Saved you days of wandering the desert like Moses; you can thank me later."

"What the hell is Doomtown?" Shane asked.

"Eat your burger; it'll get cold," the ghost gestured toward Ventura's plate before looking back at Shane. "Back when the U.S. government was doing its nuclear tests in the fifties, they built a place called Doomtown. Just a little fake neighborhood. A few mockups of homes with all the furnishings and even some mannequin families. Some cars, picket fences, real swanky. They blew up a sixteen-kiloton bomb they named Annie right down the street."

"Walter Cronkite reported on that," Ventura said. "I watched the footage once."

Coulson raised an eyebrow and then looked at Shane.

"How old is your partner?" he asked.

"He likes vintage Americana. Ask him about the mob in Vegas," Shane said.

"Anyway, the first house was blown to smithereens. Real dramatic stuff," Coulson explained. "The point was just to be sensational, show the power of the war machine, you know? People at home watching these mannequins being seared off the face of the earth and feeling secure that we can do that to our enemies."

"But it was just a handful of mannequins," Ventura said. "No one got hurt."

"Not there," Coulson agreed. "But that wasn't the only test site. Doomtown II, or Survival City, was another one. This place was bigger, with more buildings and more mannequins. Some of it's still standing. But those were the only two that got press. They also built Doomtown III."

"That one was a secret," Shane concluded.

"Big time," Coulson confirmed. "Three was the biggest. Dozens of buildings. Houses, a school, a church. Real quaint little neighborhood. Folks probably enjoyed it until they had their skins blasted off."

Ventura stared at Coulson, his burger suspended above his plate.

"You're saying they used live subjects? The government?"

"I don't know who conducted every test, and I don't know if they knew who set up every area around the test sites, but Doomtown III was not populated by mannequins."

"That's insane," Ventura said. "The government, the military, whoever, you're saying they tested nuclear weapons on citizens?"

"Oh, God. This guy plays for the home team." Coulson leaned back in his seat and ran a hand through his hair.

"It's not unprecedented. You're a history guy; you know that," Shane said.

There had been more than a few cases in the past when soldiers and even civilians had been subject to gruesome fates in the name of experiments they didn't know they were participating in.

"But I don't know this history. I've never heard this in my life," Ventura said.

"Because they kept this one covered up," Coulson said. "Easy to do when the whole place is saturated in radiation. Stops people from looking around too much."

"And this is where the radioactive haunted items are coming from," Shane said.

"This was the thing that just happened outside of Vegas, I assume? Some guy trafficking in radioactive junk for the mob? I didn't read the whole article," Coulson said. "That was you guys, right?"

"Yep," Shane said. "What are you doing here? Did you also find out about that?"

"That crossed into what I'm doing. No offense, but your thing was small potatoes. I'm here for PULSE 2."

Shane nodded and took a bite of his sandwich. He waited for Coulson to continue because he didn't want to play the game of acting interested in the ghost's cryptic statement. Ventura, on the other hand, was all in.

"What's PULSE 2?" The agent lowered his voice.

Coulson grinned at Shane and leaned in.

"Glad you asked, Xander. Like Doomtown I and II, there was a PULSE 1. Underground lab where they did some physics and nuclear testing-type experiments. Or that's the official word. I still haven't been down there, so forgive me if that's where the aliens are being kept. But PULSE 1 is just the one people know exists. PULSE 2 is the one no one knows about."

"So, how do you know? And what do they do there?" Ventura asked.

"I know because I was told. And what they do there is stuff so secret that they don't want anyone to know about it. But I have it on good authority it's not your standard math and science, you know? No one's making models of the solar system or baking soda volcanoes."

"Can you be more specific? Maybe wrap this conversation up before the sun goes down?" Shane suggested. Coulson wasn't usually this theatrical, but Shane guessed he was playing it up for Ventura's benefit. He liked showing off a little.

"Ghosts. The dead. The irradiated dead," Coulson said simply.

It was the answer Shane expected, and also entirely useless. Why would anyone irradiate haunted items? The item was dangerous, but it wasn't as though the ghost would be. It'd just be like the ones he found near Ross' ranch outside of Vegas. Badly burned and potentially homicidal, but otherwise unremarkable. Although Shane conceded that the ghost he called Night Light had developed a quirk that allowed him to glow incredibly bright in the darkness of some tunnels, that wasn't a typical ghost trait.

"So, are you like a ghost PI?" Ventura returned to his burger. Coulson looked almost offended.

"I am not a PI," he said dryly. "I fix problems other people can't."

"So what do you need us for?" Ventura asked.

Shane had also wondered about that. Coulson seemed to know a lot already. He had a lead on whatever he was looking for, and he knew the fundamentals and even where to start. What could Shane and Ventura have done for him that he could not have done for himself?

"There's more going on in that desert than it seems," Coulson replied. "I learned most of what I know from my contact; this isn't firsthand stuff."

"Who's your contact?" Shane asked.

He knew the ghost trusted Jillian, but he didn't think there were many other people in the world Thomas Coulson would take at their word as reliable sources of information. Nor would he need to when he could pick over someone's brain with his psychic abilities to learn what he needed. Having a source or contact at all seemed odd for him.

"Old friend," Coulson explained. "Someone you already know, Shane. We could go say hello if you like."

Shane finished his coffee and set the mug back on the table. He looked out the window at the desert across the street, the vast expanses of monotone emptiness broken only by the occasional bit of scraggly vegetation and distant mountains.

He and Coulson had not spent a lot of time together. The number of people that both men knew who were still alive was small. Coulson's coy tone made Shane think a joke was hidden in his statement anyway.

"Sure, let's go." Ventura pulled out his wallet to pay the bill. He slowed when he realized neither Shane nor Coulson was in a hurry to join him.

"Something wrong?" he asked.

"Still waiting for an answer." Shane looked at the ghost. "What do you need us for?"

"Isn't this the same case you're working?" Coulson asked. "You want to find where the irradiated ghosts come from, I can take you there."

"You're not a tour guide," Shane said. "I won't lie and say you haven't pulled my ass out of the fire more than once, but that was you helping me with your admittedly unique skill set and doing things I couldn't do. What can I do for you out in that desert?"

Coulson smiled and reached into his jacket. He pulled out a cigarette with a plain, yellow filter and slipped it between his lips. The tip lit on its own, but no one in the diner noticed it, or even that he was smoking.

"You have a suspicious nature, Ryan."

"And you are not good at being evasive," Shane said. "Probably never wasted much time learning the skill if you can just play around in people's thoughts. Which you aren't doing to either of us."

"It's bad form to shape the thoughts of colleagues, Ryan, even if it makes things easier," Coulson explained. "I don't spend a lot of time doing that anymore, anyway. Not since I went noncorporeal."

"You mean you lost the ability because you have to devote more energy to fooling people into thinking you're alive."

The ember on Coulson's phantom cigarette glowed a bright orange. The ghost's eyes remained locked on Shane, but it was Ventura who answered.

"Didn't lose the ability." The agent spoke Coulson's words. "Just not something I need to waste energy on unless I need to prove a point."

Ventura gasped suddenly and shook his head, released from Coulson's hold as quickly as he had been taken.

"Don't ever do that again." Ventura breathed sharply and leaned back in the booth as though putting a few inches of distance between himself and the ghost would prevent Coulson from controlling his mind again.

"Okay, point taken," Shane said, "but you're still skirting the issue. Why do you need us?"

"Come with me," Coulson said. "You'll see."

CHAPTER 3
FAMILIAR FACES

Coulson led the two men from the diner and into the desert behind it and the motel. He walked at a leisurely pace, unaffected by the sun and dry heat as he smoked a cigarette that refused to create an ash or get any smaller.

Aside from the cigarette, the only other thing that gave Coulson away as being something other than a normal man was the fact he did not leave footprints in the sand.

"Where are we going?" Ventura asked.

His interest in the ghost had waned considerably since his moment of mind control, and now, he was back to a more suspicious nature. He'd live longer with that mindset, Shane thought. If Coulson wanted their help, it was with something dangerous.

"Right there." The ghost pointed toward the horizon. A small, silver trailer sat among the cacti ahead, with an awning strung out for shade, and a scattering of chairs and benches outside.

The closer they got, the easier it was to make out the finer details. The trailer was aluminum and looked to have stood up well to life in the desert, though the windows were caked with dust and the glass looked like it hadn't been cleaned in years.

A fire pit outside the trailer had chairs around it like maybe a group of people was camping in the small thing, but there were little signs of life. The bits of garbage trapped by the trailer wheels looked months old or more, and there was little of it beyond a couple of bottles and an old bag of popcorn.

The little plot was shaded by a large tarp attached to the trailer and held up by tent poles. It wasn't all that messy; it just looked forgotten.

The aluminum door to the trailer was propped open, but an inner screen door was closed, presumably to keep insects out. It must have done nothing for the dust and certainly couldn't have kept the place cool.

With the awning casting shade on the trailer, Shane couldn't see who, if anyone, was inside. He didn't think Coulson was staying in the trailer, though. It was not his style.

"You got the Unabomber in there?" Ventura asked as they got closer.

"Not exactly," Coulson answered.

Before Ventura could ask another question, the screen door opened and a young man with long, dark hair and a tan stepped down into the sand, holding a bucket of fried chicken in one arm and a Big Gulp in the other.

Shane raised an eyebrow and the man, his mouth full of chicken, laughed raucously.

"Oh, man! I knew I'd see you again, man! This is the best. Coulson getting the band back together again!"

He set the chicken and drink on a weathered picnic table and rubbed his hands aggressively on the Guns N' Roses T-shirt that hung off his lanky frame as he approached Shane.

"How have you been, man?" he asked, his arms spread as though coming in for a hug.

Shane put a hand out and took a step back. The long-haired man stopped, nodding and laughing more as he lowered his hands.

"Personal space, man; I dig it. They didn't have that when I was here the first time around, but I get it now, and it's cool."

He turned to Ventura and shrugged, spreading his arms again and tilting his head as though silently asking for approval.

"No, thanks," Ventura said.

"Alright, man. But I dig your vibe. You're very official-looking, man. Like my guy Shane here is a cowboy and you're like… the sheriff. Very cool."

"Who are you?" Ventura asked.

Shane recognized the man from back when he first dealt with the Endless Night. He had been the first real lead Shane had in tracking down Coulson. Back then, however, the man had been staying at Jillian's house.

"Dezzy?" Shane wasn't sure if he remembered correctly.

Shane had not spent a long time with him and honestly did not want to. The man seemed trapped in a stoner movie.

"Heck yeah, man!" Dezzy grinned widely. "You guys want some chicken? I only got one Big Gulp, but you can help yourselves. It's Mountain Dew and Dr. Pepper."

"Together?" Ventura asked.

Dezzy laughed and nodded.

"Who the hell is this guy?" Ventura asked Shane.

"I don't know. He's Coulson's friend," Shane answered.

"He used to be a scion of the Prince of Nothing if that means anything to you," Coulson said, sitting at the picnic table while Dezzy joined him in the shade.

"It doesn't," Ventura said.

"He was dead. For a long time. Then he became undead," the ghost said.

"He's a zombie?"

"Don't be absurd, Agent Ventura. He's alive. A living thing can die, and a dead thing can, in some very rare circumstances, live again. That's what happened to Dezzy. But it put him in the unique position of having an affinity for death and the dead. He knows more than his admittedly silly behavior would make you think."

"For sure, man," Dezzy agreed, taking a drumstick from the bucket of chicken. "Like the soul-scorching that went on in the desert. You need an intense amount of primordial energy to do that to a soul. I haven't seen anything like it since the Void."

Shane grunted, ignoring Dezzy in favor of Coulson.

"What are we here for again?"

"Dezzy's the one who gave me the heads up about PULSE 2."

"There are some serious spiritual shenanigans happening out there. Feels like when you eat spicy food, you know? And it builds this slow burn at the back of your throat that creeps up until your mouth is on fire?" Dezzy addressed Shane and Ventura.

"Coulson," Shane said.

The ghost sighed, butting out his cigarette on the table until it vanished.

"Let them talk to the doctor," Coulson said to Dezzy.

"Oh, good thinking," Dezzy said. "He gets the sciencey stuff way better than me."

Dezzy stood and went into the trailer, leaving the door open.

"I came out here to see Queens of the Stone Age in Vegas a couple months ago," Dezzy shouted from inside as he rummaged through a cupboard. "But then I got a feeling about this place out in the desert and had to check it out."

"What do you mean a feeling?" Ventura asked.

"Like a whole vibe, you know? In my gut. Something wasn't right."

"You can sense spirits?" the agent asked.

Dezzy popped his head back out of the door and grinned.

"Oh, sure. It was more than that, though, man. This whole PULSE 2 lab doesn't even officially exist. You'll never find it on a map, and no one talks about it. If you *did* find a map, even a top-secret one, and you drew some lines to see who has jurisdiction over which parts of the desert, you'd find a tiny little triangle that no one claims."

"How do you know that?" Shane asked.

"I drew the lines, man!" Dezzy said. He handed out a rolled-up piece of paper and then returned to looking for whatever he was looking for in the trailer.

Shane unrolled the paper on the picnic table, revealing a topographical map of the Nevada Test Site that originally dated back to the fifties but had been overlaid with more current data.

As Dezzy had said, there were lines drawn on it with a ruler and handmade notes that pointed out which sections were under the banner of the Department of Energy, which were Air Force, which had been Army, and every other governing body that had claimed the land for the past seventy years. There was a single triangle of land that all the lines avoided, a no-man's-land inside a no-man's-land.

"This was never claimed by anyone?" Ventura asked.

"Outside of everyone's jurisdiction since the beginning," Coulson said. "From the outside, it looks like a big slab of empty land, but , there were maps of top-secret test sites, labs, and places like Doomtown. This is Frankensteined together from all those maps. That spot and a handful of smaller ones were never under anyone's command, but that's where the PULSE 2 lab was built."

"And no one claims ownership," Ventura said, "so everyone can deny involvement if whatever happens out there is discovered."

"Exactly," Coulson said. "Decades of deniability and secrecy. No one can be held accountable for a forgotten lab that never officially existed doing secret experiments no one has the authority to learn about."

"But someone built it. Someone ran it," Ventura said.

"*Runs* it," Coulson corrected. "There's still something happening out there."

"The PULSE 2 experiments aren't, ya know, good ones." Dezzy returned from the trailer with an old, beat-up box.

He dropped the box on the table on top of the map, and it hit with a thud. The box was heavier than it looked, and Shane already suspected what was inside.

"You'll want to move back a little," Coulson suggested.

Shane moved back, out from under the awning and back into the sun.

Ventura moved with him, slowly and cautiously, while Dezzy opened a padlock, flipped the clasp on the box, and lifted the lid.

He took his chicken and Big Gulp and stepped away from the picnic table to join Shane and Ventura. The box, as Shane had guessed, was lined with lead but thicker than he had expected. There was a human skull in the center of it, burned on one side and cracked down the center.

The ghost was slow to appear after the box was opened. When he manifested, he stood next to the box, looking down at the skull.

Like some of the ghosts Shane had seen near Bennet Ross' ranch, this one had died from severe burns. Radiation, Shane assumed. The man's face was melting. It was actively happening as Shane watched.

Flesh ran down the ghost's face like melting candle wax, mixing with blood and vitreous fluid from his burst left eye. It was a never-ending cascade of bloody, glossy, chunky sludge that rebuilt itself as quickly as it slopped down the spirit's neck and chest so that it never ran out.

The spirit was dressed only on the side that was melting. About a third of the ghost's body on the right side had been incinerated past clothing, flesh, and muscle, down to bone. The burns on the spirit matched the burns on the skull.

Despite having no eye on the right and a melting eye on the left, the ghost could see and quickly picked Dezzy out of the group.

"Why am I here, Dezzy?" His voice was strained and garbled.

"Hey, Doc. I'm sorry, man. These guys are here to help with the lab, and they just need to know some more stuff."

"Dezzy." The ghost's tired voice was almost a sigh. It seemed everyone had the same reaction to Dezzy.

"I know, Doc!" Dezzy turned to face Shane and Ventura.

"Doc asked me not to bring him out again. He's kind of radioactive and is worried about hurting people."

"Not 'kind of,'" the ghost said. "Even in death, I am poison. I should be sealed in that lead box and dropped into a salt mine for the rest of time."

27

Ventura took a notable step back, further into the blistering sun.

"How radioactive?"

Doc made a humming sound and shook his head, causing the melting flesh to dribble faster.

"I can't accurately read anything without instruments. Based on the research I was doing in my lab, you're absorbing ten to fifteen millisieverts every minute you're exposed to my skull."

Ventura looked at Shane and raised an eyebrow.

"Couple of CT scans, I think," Shane said.

"Every minute?"

"Then you should talk fast," Shane said as Ventura backed off again.

He was killing them just by being there.

CHAPTER 4

THE CUTTING EDGE

"I ran the PULSE 2 weapons lab in nineteen seventy-two. Dezzy tells me that was... a few years ago," Doc said.

The ghost stood next to his skull, his body hunched and tired looking beyond the horrible disfigurements he'd endured.

"It was a while, man," Dezzy confirmed.

"We had discovered in the early sixties that death by acute exposure to radiation had potentially damning effects on post-biological entities."

"Post-biological entities," Coulson interrupted with a chuckle. He was smoking a new cigarette and pointing his thumb at Doc. "That's what they called ghosts."

"Ghosts." Doc's voice bubbled like he had deep congestion. "This was all cutting-edge work, totally unprecedented and totally off the books. The very idea that... ghosts were real was not something any of us had encountered in any field of science. It was quackery. Delusional thinking. Or so everyone thought."

"Who proved you wrong? Who was running this lab?" Ventura asked.

"It was a government contract. I was told it was the Air Force's nuclear weapons center. But I later heard some were contracted by the Department of Energy, and there were some from the Department of Defense. I started to believe none of these were official."

"So you don't know who hired you. Or who signed your checks," Ventura said.

"This was top-secret work," Doc said. "You don't ask to see your boss' ID and work history when you're developing nuclear weapons technology that defies the very fabric of science."

"What weapons?" Shane asked to get them back on track. "What were you doing to ghosts?"

Shane knew more than the average person about ghosts and how they functioned, but he knew little about ghosts born from radiation. He had never seen evidence that the cause of death altered the ghost very much. Some, like Doc, wound up looking awful. Some were more dangerous and unstable than others. But that was personality and how their minds functioned, or didn't function.

"You know the dead." Doc nodded at Shane. "You're different from Mr. Coulson and Dezzy here. You have seen them for a long time, yes?"

"Yes," Shane confirmed.

Doc smiled, or tried as well as he could given the state of his face.

"We had a man like you in the lab. Lamb was his name. David, I think. David Lamb. Our post-biological expert. They called him a non-traditional. A Delta. So many code words. He was a behaviorist. He told us what to expect. And eventually, he had nothing to tell us, because we broke all the rules he thought he knew."

"Doc, you're literally killing us going through this backstory," Shane said. "Can we get to the point?"

The ghost grumbled and nodded.

"The universe is arranged around fundamental forces," the ghost said. "Everything is beholden to them. Gravity, electromagnetism, and the strong and weak nuclear forces. Do you know about this?"

"I went to high school," Shane said.

"But they never taught you this. The weak nuclear force is particle decay, hmm? Neutrinos turn into electrons, and our sun's fusion reaction keeps on churning. And strong nuclear force! Strongest power in the universe. Holds atoms together."

"You're losing them, Doc," Dezzy interrupted. "You should skip to the experiments."

30

The melting ghost grunted again and shrugged.

"Yes, yes. There is a force within the post-biological entity. There is something that makes a ghost a ghost. No atoms any more, but a force nonetheless. And it is stripped from the biological source, from the material source, at the moment of death. We discovered, based on earlier data that had been observed by chance, that when a sufficient radioactive force is applied to a biologic that the ghost stripped away, at the critical moment of transfer, it can carry over traits of the radioactive force that caused the transfer."

Doc was smiling again, an unnerving expression as his oozing flesh dribbled past his lips. Shane ran a hand across his head and pulled out a cigarette from his pocket, lighting it while squinting against the sun.

"You killed people by exposing them to radiation to make irradiated ghosts?" he asked finally.

"In so many words," Doc replied. "It was very experimental. Very difficult to control. It is not easy to make a ghost, and we never learned what prompted their growth."

"Pain," Ventura said. "Extreme trauma and pain will do it nine times out of ten."

Ventura and Shane had dealt with a group called the Harvesters, who had refined a technique to guarantee a ghost's creation. It involved some of the worst torture Shane had seen, plus the influence of a second ghost. But if a ghost introduced at the moment of death could ensure a new ghost for the Harvesters, had the PULSE lab rats found a way to ensure radiation was somehow part of a ghost's makeup? What the hell did that even mean?

"There was pain," Doc said softly, looking at his melting hand.

"Did you succeed?" Shane asked, not interested in the ghost's self-pity for whatever pain he'd caused. "Did you make ghosts, not just haunted items, that are radioactive?"

"Some," Doc said. "We used extreme gamma and alpha particle exposure. Most of the subjects died quickly and left nothing behind. I learned new things every day to keep up. I had barely begun to understand what a ghost was, and we were tasked with making them mobile, controllable nuclear weapons."

"What does that mean?" Ventura asked. "How do you turn a ghost into a nuclear weapon?"

"Post-biological entities have an environmental control factor that defied study. They can dim lights. They lower the temperature in a given space through some unknown energy transfer. But they are the conduits for this energy transfer, and it seems to be conscious. Our goal was to make radiation another factor controlled by them."

"So instead of making a room cold when they show up, they make it radioactive and kill whatever's there. You can send one into an enemy base and give everyone radiation poisoning without having to expose a living soldier from your side to any danger," Shane said.

"Yes." Doc nodded. "That's exactly what we were trying to do."

"And it worked," Shane added.

"The results were not as good as we had hoped. That it worked at all was astonishing. We had developed nearly two dozen by the time of the accident."

"Your accident?" Shane asked.

"A loss of containment. One of the entities escaped and caused a chain reaction. I don't know if the other labs were contained. I... did not survive."

"A ghost did this to you?" Ventura asked. "Killed you and made your body too dangerous to even be out in the open?"

"Yes." Doc nodded.

"Jesus," Ventura said. "What happened to it?"

"I did not survive," Doc repeated. "My body was dumped in the desert, too far for me to return to the lab. But it's still out there. Still operational. The work never ended. I can't imagine what progress has been made in half a century."

Shane puffed out a cloud of smoke and turned to look back the way they had come, across the empty desert and the distant mountains past the diner.

"So it's not just radioactive skeletons; radioactive ghosts are out there. And they're weaponized."

"That was our primary goal," Doc conceded. "Our success was limited. Rudimentary and impossible to control. But if the work continued, then it stands to reason their successes made it worth the effort."

"That's insane," Ventura said. "How many people did you kill? How many innocent people did you murder to create these weapons?"

Doc cocked his head quizzically, and the oozing fluids dribbled onto his shoulder.

"There were no murders, sir." The ghost's voice was even thicker now. "These were volunteers."

Shane pulled the cigarette from between his lips and raised his eyebrow.

"They volunteered to be burned to death with radiation?"

"To become weapons," Doc agreed. "I spoke extensively with all the participants. Many of them watched the process before consenting to join. They knew what was happening."

"No." Ventura shook his head. "Not a chance. One fanatic, maybe. Hell, maybe two or three. How many did you do this to?"

"We had a test group of seventy-two. All aware, and all of sound mind. They chose to become weapons, sir. Burnt Souls, the others took to calling them. To harness the most destructive power mankind has developed and control it with their minds. Forever. To be beyond death and all-powerful. Many of these volunteers believed they were becoming something close to a god."

Ventura scoffed, but Shane exhaled a slow puff of smoke and considered the ghost's words. He didn't like the implications of a radioactive ghost created from someone expecting otherworldly powers.

The thing that Doc and the rest of his team probably had not accounted for was something beyond the process of stripping a soul from a mortal body. Ghosts did not come back as the same person every time. Not even most of the time, in Shane's experience. Dying had a severe and unpredictable effect on the human psyche. Creating a broken spirit with the power to melt living people just by being near them was a catastrophically bad idea.

"I need to go away now. It's not safe for me to be out here any longer," Doc said.

He looked at Ventura then, his half-melted eye still somehow seeing him.

"Trust that whatever monster you think I am, I have thought the same thing about myself. I'll pay for what I did for a long while, but at the time, I thought I was helping. I thought I was making our country safe by helping to defend it against our enemies."

The ghost looked at Dezzy, and the younger man set down a chicken thigh and reached for the lead box.

"See you later, Doc," he said.

He closed the box, and the ghost vanished. Dezzy secured it so that it couldn't open by accident and then carried it back inside the trailer while Coulson leaned back and spread his arms.

"There you go. The long and short of it."

"You've seen these radioactive ghosts?" Shane asked.

Coulson shook his head.

"No. I found the off-the-books Doomtown, and that place had a lot of dead, but no supervillain types. They were scared, though. Something's been clear-cutting the dead out there."

"Were they volunteers?" Ventura asked.

"No," Coulson said. "Not the Doomtown dead. But give Doc a break on that one; he wasn't involved in whatever happened there. This place has layers like an onion. That triangle, that little unaffiliated chunk of land

34

no one was responsible for, was the Wild West. Anything goes. No rules, and no oversight."

"So why is anything happening now? This lab has been running in secret since the seventies. What went wrong?" Ventura asked.

"Something happened, but I don't know what. People have even been clearing out the evidence. Your guy in Vegas with his irradiated dead is just one of them. It's bigger than all that, but whatever is holding it all together is lost on me right now."

"How is any of this lost on you?" Shane asked.

It was one thing for there to be a coverup and a mystery relating to experiments in the desert. That part made the most sense to Shane. But Coulson needing his help, and not being able to put the pieces together, was something unexpected.

"Yeah." Coulson put out his cigarette on the table as Dezzy returned from the trailer. "Thing about that is related to what Doc said. There's a point where radiation and how I hold myself together don't agree with each other."

"Your power doesn't work out there?" Shane asked.

"I can function, but I lose the Sight sometimes because I need to focus more energy on holding myself together. Other times, it's like static on an old TV, and I can't sense what I should be able to. I can't track down these ghost nukes if I'm fumbling in the dark half the time," Coulson said.

"So you're just a regular guy out there. You're like us." Shane nodded to Ventura.

"No," Coulson said. "I'm still better than you two. Just limited compared to how I should be."

"You're humble, I'll give you that," Ventura said.

"Just being honest, Agent Ventura. I'm good at what I do. So good, in fact, that I know when I need backup."

"Everyone needs backup sometimes," Ventura said, but it was hard to tell if he was agreeing with Coulson or taking a dig at him.

"Sure do. Who's Astrid, by the way?" Coulson tilted his head in thought.

Ventura did not answer. Shane had not heard the name before. It was nothing the agent had brought up with him, but judging by the way the color drained from his face and his body tensed, Coulson had touched a nerve.

"Are we doing this, or what?" Ventura asked.

"Let me take you to Doomtown. I'll catch you up to speed with everything I've seen," Coulson said. "Then we can start looking for whatever's out there that's got even the dead scared."

CHAPTER 5

DOOMTOWN

Shane and Ventura briefly returned to the motel to get some supplies. Shane opted for a bottle of water and a fresh pack of cigarettes while Ventura made sure he was equipped with enough iron weapons to fend off any ghosts if they were attacked, including a pair of bags loaded with iron shavings that he jammed haphazardly into his pockets. Coulson, of course, needed nothing.

Dezzy opted to stay at Doc's trailer. It seemed like he was just living out there now, despite having admitted to stumbling upon the situation by accident on a trip to Las Vegas. Dezzy was a man who lived by the seat of his pants.

"We'll have to walk before long," Coulson said when they were ready to go. "I think motion detectors monitor the area. They're not triggered by humans or smaller animals, seems to just be vehicles. I had Dezzy do a few test runs with me."

"How far can we drive?" Ventura asked.

"A few miles. We can get past the main fence and the guard station, but another few miles in, we'll have to ditch the car to be safe. Doomtown's probably the best place to do it. It'll provide some cover in case anyone comes looking, too."

"How do we get past the guards?"

"We'll ask nicely," Coulson said. "Don't worry about it."

Shane followed directions from Coulson and took them less than a mile down the road from Benton to a slightly flatter than normal patch of sand the ghost insisted was a road. It was hard to discern from the rest of the desert, but Shane took the turn nonetheless and drove them out into the empty Mojave.

In short order, they found themselves unable to see anything ahead or behind save for sand, sun, and rocks. Patches of scrub and cacti dotted the landscape, and sometimes, they passed impressive piles of boulder and stone but not much else.

After fifteen minutes of driving, something appeared on the horizon. What was at first just a dark line became clearer. It was a fence, spanning as far as Shane could see in either direction.

Despite there still being no sign they were on an established road, Coulson had not been wrong. They were headed toward a gate, fixed in place behind a small, shack-like guard station.

Two armed men in military uniforms blocked their path as they approached. One of them entered the small guard shack, and the other remained out front. Neither was aiming his weapon, but they were within reach, and Shane was certain they were trained to use them if necessary.

"This will just take a moment," Coulson said.

Shane slowed the car as Coulson, in the passenger seat, leaned over Shane toward the driver's side window. As obnoxious as it was, Shane let him do it. He was more focused on the two guards than what the ghost was doing. There were no patches on the men's uniforms. No rank insignias, and nothing that indicated even what branch of the military they were supposed to be in.

Aside from the desert camo pattern, nothing about them made them official in any way. They could have been two guys in Halloween costumes, if not for the fact that their guns were very real.

As if to mock Shane's thoughts, the guard in the station raised the rifle to his shoulder, pointing the barrel at him as the other guard held up his hand and approached the car.

"You need to head back. This is a restricted area," the man said.

Ventura shifted in the backseat, and Shane knew he had his gun ready but hidden.

"We're supposed to head inside. We're inspecting the lab today," Coulson said. "Open the gate."

"Open the gate," said the guard who had just told them to leave.

The man in the booth nodded and lowered his weapon. He pressed a button, and the gate pulled back on small, squealing wheels, allowing them to pass through. There was no hesitation or questioning from either of them. Coulson might as well have been a four-star general giving orders.

Coulson leaned back in his seat and gestured forward.

"Get moving," he said to Shane.

Shane put his foot on the gas, and they started moving. The gate rolled shut behind them, and the two guards didn't give them a second look.

"So much for not having all your abilities," Shane said. "That was a hell of a Jedi mind trick."

"Out here," Coulson said. "Once we get where we're going, that's the problem. It clings to me like tar. Takes hours to thin out enough so I can regain focus and do things like that again. Don't expect too many miracles when we're in the thick of it."

"Does that mean they're going to realize they were duped and come after us?" Ventura looked out on the rear windshield.

"No. They won't even remember seeing us within the next five minutes," the ghost replied.

Coulson directed Shane off the road that he still couldn't fully see. He had them heading northeast, using landmarks like an unusually tall cactus and a pile of rocks that looked like a sleeping dog. None of it made sense until they were close enough and Shane saw what the ghost meant. No one could have followed Coulson's directions if he hadn't been there to clarify them.

Soon enough, they entered a shallow valley that was partially bordered by a hill on the southern side. Within the valley as they headed down from the hilltop, Shane saw a random assembly of structures. It looked like a town that someone had started to build and then given up on very quickly. A small number of houses, a church, and even a gas station and a schoolhouse, but not much else.

There were perhaps a dozen houses, built to nearly identical standards, lined up on two streets though there were no pavement or sidewalks.

"Welcome to Doomtown," Coulson said as Shane slowed the vehicle.

He pulled the car into the driveway of the closest house, parking it like it was meant to be there alongside a dusty, once-white picket fence. Everything in town looked like it had once been colorful and vibrant. Blue and yellow paint jobs were under years of dust and sun bleaching.

Shane got out of the car and stood in the heat of the sun, squinting down the street. Coulson had said Doomtown was full of ghosts, but he couldn't see any. Instead, he was struck by the stillness of the place. It was as quiet as a grave.

Perhaps because of the shallow valley, the wind did not touch the place, and everything felt frozen and forgotten in time. The sand crunching under Shane's boots when he moved seemed too loud like it would draw the attention of everyone in town had anyone been there to hear it.

"This place has been here since the fifties?" Ventura asked.

"Near as I can tell," Coulson said. "There were more ghosts here last time. Hidden in the houses but watching from windows."

"I don't see anyone," Ventura said.

"Yeah," Coulson agreed. "Something changed."

The ghost passed through the fence and walked to the door of the house, pushing it open. Shane followed, lifting his leg to get over the small fence and crunching across the sandy patch that served as a front lawn.

Inside the house was somehow both more and less than Shane expected. Someone had taken the time to add furnishings like a sofa and chair set in the living room, and a dining set off the kitchen. But even under all the layers of dust, it had a fake quality to it. Nothing looked lived-in about the house, which made the staging seem oddly pointless.

Decades of being alone in the desert had rendered the house lifeless in every sense of the word. The dust had sapped the color from everything so it was monotone beige, gray, and faded brown. It looked like the memory of something rather than anything real.

Coulson went up the stairs while Shane remained on the ground floor. He opened some of the cupboard doors in the kitchen, pushing aside dusty glasses and old soup cans that had survived more than half a century and were probably radioactive enough to kill anyone who dared eat them.

A family of mannequins sat around the dining table, with place settings in front of each. Everyone had a plate, a fork, a knife, a spoon, and a glass. None of the mannequins bore a face.

"Why do you think they put the mannequins here?" Ventura joined Shane in the dining room. "If this was a place to experiment on people, what's the point?"

"For us," Shane said. "Anyone who came after to wonder why they put mannequins if this place was meant for the living. Makes it seem like maybe you're wrong. Maybe there were never living people here. Little details make a coverup more believable."

"Is it a coverup if no one knows about it?" Ventura asked.

"That's the best kind," Shane told him. "Like an ace up your sleeve just in case. After this many years, no one would believe anything happened here because no one heard anything."

"You're very cynical," Ventura said.

"That would hit harder if we weren't investigating a program meant to turn irradiated ghosts into weapons."

"There's no one here." Coulson came down the stairs. "This place was full of ghosts when I was here before. Dozens of them."

"Maybe they saw us coming and are hiding," Ventura suggested.

"Ghosts can't hide from me," Coulson said on the way out the door.

Shane and Ventura followed him outside as he took a sharp left and headed down the street, passing the houses and the church toward the open desert again.

"He seems angry," Ventura whispered as they started to follow.

"A little," Shane said. The ghost was four buildings ahead of them and making a beeline toward nothing at all from what Shane saw. "Or he's afraid of something."

"You know him better than I do. You think he gets scared?"

"Not until just now," Shane admitted. "Coulson usually makes me nervous."

"Really?" Ventura let out a quick chuckle. "Didn't think any ghost could do that to you."

"He's not any ghost," Shane said. "I fought him before. He's tough, Xander. My fists, iron, nothing stops him."

"What do you mean iron doesn't stop him?" Ventura asked, all the mirth stripped from his voice. Now it was Shane's turn to laugh.

"All this time he's been moving around with us, and you never wondered where his haunted item was?"

The realization only dawned on Ventura as Shane mentioned it.

"I don't get it. How can he move this far without it?"

"There is no 'it'," Shane said. "*He's* it. He's bound to himself. He could travel around the world."

"So if you hit him with iron, he goes nowhere?"

"Might as well hit him with a Nerf bat," Shane confirmed.

"And you can't destroy him?"

"Our fight didn't go that far. I don't know."

"Of course, he can't destroy me. Why would I let him do that?" Coulson shouted from a few yards ahead of them.

He had stopped walking and was now just standing over something, away from the houses and the fakery of Doomtown. Shane and Ventura joined him at the ledge of a wide hole.

At first, it looked to Shane like someone had dug out the foundation for a new home and had struck a cavern in the rock. There was a hole within the hole, a place where the stone had collapsed into a dark cave. It must have been like the tunnels under Bennet Ross' ranch. But the rest of the hole, the part that hadn't collapsed, was peppered with dusty bits of old fabric and a few small, scattered bones. Most were finger joints, and there was a whole foot as well, but nothing more substantial.

"This was where they buried the bodies," Coulson said. "All but a few that had been pulled out recently were here. That was four days ago."

"Couldn't have been Ross and his guys who dug it up," Ventura said.

Bennett Ross and his crew were in custody. There would be no more harvesting of radioactive haunted items for him for a while.

"I don't think anyone dug it up," Shane said.

He circled the pit and crouched over the hole that led into a dark cavern below. While the wind had probably smoothed out the sand in the days since Coulson had been there, it couldn't do the same for the rock.

Shane leaned forward and pressed his hand against the edge of the opening, allowing his fingers to slip easily into four grooves that had been dug into the stone.

"That's a handprint," Ventura said. The grooves were a little wider than Shane's fingers, but the other man was right. It looked like a human hand had dug into the rock and gouged a perfect outline.

"Someone dug into this from below," Shane said. "And it looks like they used their bare hands."

CHAPTER 6
THE BLINDING LIGHT

The silence of Doomtown had become deafening. If something underground had dragged away the dead, something was happening well beyond men trafficking in radioactive haunted items and even weaponized ghosts in the desert. It didn't fit with anything Shane had heard. He didn't have a lot of feasible explanations for what he saw.

"Can you sense anything here?" Shane asked.

Coulson couldn't keep the scowl from his face as he looked back at the town.

"No. It's murky here in a way it wasn't on my first pass. I can't see it the way I used to."

"They could still be here then, couldn't they? Some of them?" Ventura asked.

"There were skeletons here," Coulson assured him. "No one dragged those back to the houses. But yeah, maybe a few are left behind. Ones who never got tossed here in the first place. I don't know."

Shane felt the stress in the ghost's voice. He was trying to be cool about it; nonchalant, even. But Thomas Coulson did not like being hobbled. He didn't like that there were things he didn't know.

"We should search the town. Split up, go building to building, and stay within shouting distance until the full thing is swept and we know one way or another. Our best bet to figure out what's going on is to find one of these ghosts, not one who's been in a trailer since the Nixon administration," Ventura suggested.

There were hours of sunlight left, and they were within a triangle of map that no one claimed. It was as good a time as any for them to see what else they could discover. Shane didn't have a lot of faith that someone had overlooked a ghost, but he didn't have a better idea at that moment, either.

"I'll take the far side of town." Shane nodded back toward where they had parked.

"I'll start here." Ventura headed toward the closest house.

Coulson said nothing, looking into the hole in the earth again before turning his back on it and heading toward Doomtown's mockup of a church.

Shane watched Ventura disappear into the first house and continued up the street to where the car was parked. Across from the house they had first entered was another identical structure, this one painted in a faded pink that, after so many years, looked like a soft brown.

The inside of this house was nearly the same as the first. The Doomtown builders were not creative, although this one only had a family of three mannequins at the dinner table. There was a place setting and a seat for the fourth, but it was not present.

Shane looked in the closet and the bathroom on the first floor then headed up the stairs. Two bedrooms and another bathroom awaited him on the second floor, each one sparsely decorated to mimic reality. Someone had even made the bed in the first room.

Shane found the missing mannequin in the second room, a master bedroom. It was neatly tucked into bed, the sheets and blanket pulled tight around it. The covers extended up to the neck below the dusty, featureless face.

No spirits awaited him. Nothing in the bathroom or under the beds. He left it behind and headed to the next house in the line.

Under the layers of dust, the next house had a pastel green paint job. Inside was a carbon copy of the first two. The color of the sofa was slightly different, and the area rugs were different, but everything else was a meticulous reproduction of what he'd already seen. All four mannequins were at the dinner table, and the cupboards were mostly empty, save for a handful of random plates and cans.

Shane investigated two more houses before something new caught his eye. He was on his way out of what might have once been a yellow house, based on some of the flaking paint around the window frames, when he happened to look back at the step at the front door.

A panel of siding had slipped away at the base of the house at some point. From the way it slumped, Shane saw a space under the house. It was not large enough to be considered a crawl space, but the houses hadn't been built flat on the desert sand. Shane saw a pair of white eyes watching him from the shadows beyond the crack in the wood.

"Hey," Shane said, making eye contact. "You happen to know where everyone in town went?"

The ghost scuttled back quickly, vanishing beneath the house, and Shane sighed audibly. He approached the broken siding and crouched, pulling the panel away from where it met the front steps.

He had to lay on his stomach with his head cocked to see the space under the house. There wasn't even a foot of room below it, certainly nothing a living person could get into, but there was more than enough room for a ghost to hide.

Shane saw the shape of the spirit several feet from the edge of the house. It was cowering in the shadows, but the little bit of sunlight that came in through the missing panel showed that the ghost had been nearly reduced to a skeleton. Like some of the others Shane had seen, much of the ghost's flesh had melted away. Bits of it hung from the spirit's face and arms.

"Go away." The ghost's hiss was little more than a whisper.

"Do you know what happened to the bodies at the edge of town?" Shane asked.

"You need to leave. Now," the ghost insisted.

Its half-melted, blind eyes stared into Shane's, and the ruined flesh around its jaws stretched as it spoke. It pushed deeper into the darkness to get away from him.

"We will, but we have to find—"

"You need to leave!" the ghost insisted.

"If you could—"

"You need to leave! You need to leave! YOU NEED TO LEAVE!"

The ghost's pleading grew louder, shouting the words and clenching its bony hands into fists. Shane continued talking to it, to explain himself or even ask for the simplest information but the ghost only repeated itself, insisting that he needed to leave, its voice panicked and desperate.

Shane backed away from the panel he'd removed and got to his feet while the ghost continued to banish him from its hiding place. Talking to the ghost would be fruitless. If it had the ability to be coherent, it wasn't making much use of it. If nothing else, it proved that there could still be others in town.

A shout from down the street pulled his attention from the angry ghost. It was not a spirit; it was Ventura. Shane could not see him, but the cry was not one just to get Shane's attention. It was fear and surprise.

Shane ran toward the last place he had seen Ventura. From somewhere beyond the mock gas station, a light was building. Shane could see it rise above the rooftop like someone was increasing the output on a spotlight.

A bubble of pure, white light grew brighter from the far side of the building until it became hard to look at. Shane lowered his head, running forward toward the light.

"Ventura!" He raised a hand to block the blinding rays.

The town was still unearthly quiet. Whatever the source of the light, it made no sound, but Ventura was not replying.

Shane reached the edge of the gas station and paused. The street ahead was flooded with white light, making the desert sand look like flour and bleaching the walls of the houses on the far side of the street a stark white.

"Ryan, where are you?" Ventura shouted from somewhere within the light.

Shane gritted his teeth, leaving the protection of the gas station walls and running into the light-flooded street.

It was impossible to see what was ahead. Shane's arm provided almost no shield at all, even pressed to his forehead as he squinted below it. A low whine filled the silence, getting louder as the light grew brighter.

Shane cursed as he felt the heat build against his arm and atop his head. The glare grew hotter until it felt like flames licking at him.

"Ventura!" he yelled again.

The words vanished in the sound that accompanied the light, growing louder and more fierce. It was impossible to see where he was going. Everything around Shane was bleached white. He couldn't even see his feet, and the burning sensation was fast becoming unbearable.

Shane pulled his jacket over his head and hunched low, stumbling to one side in search of a wall and a place he could take cover. The heat penetrated the material, cut through his jeans, and seared into his boots.

With one hand blindly reaching for anything, Shane found the wall of the fake church. He moved quickly, pressing his body against it as a guide as he left the light and sound behind.

The relief from the heat was instant, but it took several seconds for his eyes to adjust. The afterimage—a purple, formless glow—saturated everything he looked at as he fell to the ground.

Light continued to blaze down the road at his left, and the sound was growing closer. Shane blinked his eyes clear and focused on his arm and hands to see if the heat had caused any serious damage. It was hard to tell, and he thought his flesh might have reddened, but there was no serious blistering.

The roaring fire sound grew louder, and he could hear nothing else. Soon, it would reach the edge of the church wall and he'd be exposed again, subject to the blinding light and heat.

There was no sign of Coulson or Ventura. He called for them but couldn't even hear his voice over the roar.

Shane stayed in a low crouch and ran to the far side of the church, ducking around the corner and putting the building between himself and whatever was coming.

The ground had begun to vibrate. Not an earthquake, but the rumble of something large and powerful nearby. It matched the deafening roar, and Shane wondered if it was what had caved in the tunnel beneath the dead. There was no way for him to tell. The light was far too bright to see anything.

The wall of the church began to rumble against Shane's back. The searing white light appeared next to him. Whatever was producing it had stepped out onto the street past the front of the church. The buildings across the street, the sand of the road, everything was washed away. Only the white remained, and the sound was louder than ever.

Shane reached into his pockets and pulled out the iron rings held within. He would not have time to fight a ghost under the conditions in Doomtown. But maybe, if it got close enough, he could get in for one clean punch. All he had to do was hit it once.

The ground shook more violently, and the church creaked at his back. The light crept beyond the wall and came toward him as the source came closer. Shane closed his eyes, balling his hands into fists as he waited. Once it reached the edge of the church next to him, he'd make his move. If it was close enough, he'd be able to endure the heat.

"Come on, you bastard." The words were barely audible in the roar of the blaze. "Let's see what you've got."

CHAPTER 7
INTO THE CRUCIBLE

With his eyes closed, all Shane saw was red. The light penetrating his eyelids washed his senses with glowing crimson like his blood was on fire. Even squeezed as tightly shut as he could get them, the light forced its way through. He felt the heat rising and knew that whatever ghost was causing it was in range. It was time to strike.

The glow flickered. Shane paused, his body tensed and ready to go. The light dimmed significantly, and the heat on his face faded.

Carefully, with a hand raised just in case, Shane opened his eyes.

"The hell are you waiting for, a written invitation?" a familiar voice yelled.

Coulson stood on the street in front of the church, his hands sunk up to the knuckles inside the skull of a glowing, white spirit. The light was severely diminished, but it was still hard to focus on the ghost. It was as though it was made of light in the shape of a human.

The glowing ghost had Coulson by the wrists and was prying his hands out of his head. It made no noise save for the roaring sound of fire that seemed to come from its body.

Coulson struggled with it, moving and bending to retain his grip as it fought like an animal to get away. He sunk his hands deeper, and the light seemed to pull from the ghost's body, drawing into Coulson's like water flowing down a drain.

The ghost became more defined, and Shane saw a pitted skeleton, its bones speckled with holes like cigarette burns. Coulson's jaw was clenched, and flakes of his body were peeling away like bits of burning tissue paper.

Shane removed the rings and approached the ghost. The empty skull gave no sign it could see Shane or that it cared about his presence. It was concerned with fighting off Coulson and nothing more.

"Move your hands when I say," Shane said.

"Just do it," Coulson growled between clenched teeth.

Shane set his hands on the pitted skull just below Coulson's. It felt hot like a rock in the desert sun, but he didn't let go. Instead, he squeezed as hard as he could. The bone began to crack. Coulson pulled away at the last moment, and Shane felt the spectral bone collapse in his grip.

With an audible snap, the ghost's head exploded. The blast wave hit Shane like a baseball bat across the chest and lifted him off his feet. He fell backward, landing harshly in the sand.

The sky above his head had a visible purple aura, the afterglow of the ghost on his retinas, and Shane stared up at it as he caught his breath. He sat up slowly, focused on his surroundings, and saw Coulson half a block away. The ghost had absorbed more of the blast than Shane had.

"Coulson?" Shane shouted.

"That was a terrible idea," the ghost shouted back.

"Where's Ventura?"

"Not sure."

Shane got to his feet, feeling unsteady as a full-body sensation of pins and needles overwhelmed him and he nearly fell over again. His pulse was racing, and if he didn't focus on something, his vision slowly drifted like his head was gently rolling to one side.

He had to stand still, breathe calmly, and wait for his body to balance itself out before he found Ventura. Coulson had yet to stand, and Shane was not sure if the ghost explosion had permanently damaged him. If it had, Shane could do nothing to help him, anyway.

"Ventura," he shouted, his head swimming with the effort.

"I'm here! I'm alive. I think," came the reply from the far side of the street.

Shane scanned the buildings and saw the FBI agent come to the door of one of the houses, his body caked in dust, cut through with lines of sweat on his face and arms.

"What the hell was that?" he asked.

Shane headed toward Coulson, still laid out on the street, as Ventura stumbled down the walkway through the picket fence gate to join him.

"Think that was one of Doc's experiments. The Burnt Souls or whatever he called them."

"So there are more of them," Ventura said.

Shane nodded, coming to a stop next to Coulson. Doc had said they had made seventy-two of them if he remembered correctly. If that was true, and they were all loose, they would need to come up with a new strategy quickly. There was no way he could take on another one of those without Coulson's help, and it looked like Coulson couldn't do it again, either.

"You alive?" Shane asked, looking down at the ghost.

"No." Coulson stared up at the sky and then Shane.

"What happened?"

"We exploded. You were there," Coulson answered.

"This is serious," Ventura interrupted.

Coulson smiled, and a cigarette appeared between his lips as though it grew from his mouth. He exhaled a puff of smoke and lifted his hand, pulling the cigarette away.

"Thank you, Agent Ventura. I hadn't realized."

He sat up quickly and got back to his feet, needlessly dusting off his clothes, which held no dust.

"You're not looking your best," Coulson said to Shane, who shrugged.

"Guess we all weathered that storm about the same. I'll be fine."

Coulson looked toward where the ghost had been and ran a hand through his hair.

"That was harder than it should have been."

"You expected it to be easy?" Ventura asked.

Coulson placed the cigarette back between his lips and nodded.

"Honestly? Yeah."

Ventura, despite having heard about Coulson, did not yet understand him. Shane understood him well enough to know it was not a good sign that Coulson had struggled with the glowing ghost. It was bad for Coulson but worse for the other two men. At least Coulson was already dead. He had a bit less to lose if a fight went wrong. At least nothing he hadn't lost once already.

"Are you okay to keep going?" Shane asked.

He didn't say out loud what he was thinking, and Coulson didn't need him to. The look he gave Shane confirmed he knew what the other man meant.

"Yeah, I'm not going anywhere," Coulson said. "But we need to get to the lab and find a way to shut these guys down, if there is one."

"They have to have haunted items still, right?" Ventura said. "Find where they're kept, and we can seal them up. If they were making radioactive ghosts, there's no way they don't have some lead-lined boxes or even rooms."

"If we can get to the items rather than the ghosts, yeah," Shane agreed. "Got a feeling it won't be as easy as all that, though."

"Look on the bright side," Coulson said. "We could have all just been vaporized, but we weren't. I'd say we're still ahead of this thing."

Coulson headed toward the road next to where the glowing ghost had first appeared. It extended half a block and then ended as the shallow valley rose in a slight hill and then trailed off into the desert.

"That ghost was definitely not here on my first visit." Coulson walked slowly past the bank with his head down.

"That's glass," Ventura said, joining the ghost.

He crouched in the sand and used the end of his iron baton to poke at the ground. The Burnt Soul had left footprints scorched into the sand that had melted into beads of glass that formed the shape of feet.

"How hot does something have to be to melt sand?" Ventura asked.

"Three thousand degrees, give or take," Shane said.

"He was that hot?" The agent looked up.

"Not when I got to him." Shane shrugged. "But I couldn't even look at him before Coulson got hands on him."

"I don't have much of a thermometer these days," Coulson admitted, "but he was putting out some energy. Felt like wind and gravity pushing on me at the same time. Like it might squash me if I let it."

"That's hotter than the melting point of iron," Ventura observed. "I've made some weapons. I'd barely be able to use them if I had to fight one of these things."

"I wouldn't worry about your weapons," Coulson said. "You'd die long before you got a chance to use them."

Ventura stood and dusted himself off, and Shane kicked at the beads of glass with the toe of his boot.

"At the end, yeah. But he was building," Shane said. "The light and the heat, even the sound. It was like an engine warming up. If we let them build to full power, we're dead. But if we can get to them before they're firing on all cylinders, we might have a chance."

"So, if it happens again, we're running in, guns blazing," Ventura said.

"Shock and awe," Coulson agreed. "I do like decisive action."

As long as there aren't several of them at a time, Shane thought.

After getting some water from the car, the three men headed into the desert, following the footprints as far as they could. The glass beads soon faded, but the ghost had left a trail that the wind had yet to sweep away. Shane saw nothing in the distance that led to where the tracks originated. The ghost must have started walking long before the trio arrived in Doomtown. Its attack appeared to be a coincidence, not something targeted.

The breeze blew hot, but there was no sign of any more of the Burnt

Souls in the open desert. The trail eventually vanished, but Coulson kept them on course, insisting he knew where the ghost had come from. Shane saw no cause to question him.

They spoke little as they walked. Ventura was breathing heavily, sweat turning the dust covering his face to mud. Coulson continued to smoke his phantom cigarettes and stay a pace or two ahead of the living men.

Shane suspected the ghost didn't want to talk about anything that had happened in the town. No one wanted to address their shortcomings or weaknesses at the best of times, and this seemed like a big blow to Coulson. One even he hadn't predicted would be as bad as it was.

"There," Coulson said after they had walked for a half hour on the Burnt Soul's trail.

"Is it the lab?" Ventura asked.

Shane squinted against the light to see a small structure on the horizon. He didn't know what they were looking for, but he wouldn't have guessed what he saw was the entrance to an important lab where many people conducted experiments. It looked like a utility shed.

A second, smaller building sat near it, with no sign of any vehicles or roads leading to either.

"That is not the PULSE lab," Coulson said.

"What is it?" Shane asked.

"I have no idea."

The lack of knowledge didn't stop them. Whatever it was, the Burnt Soul had started its journey there. Or it had at least made a pit stop.

As they got closer, Shane was better able to make out what he saw. The main structure was a door set into a cement frame, marking an entrance to something underground. The wall behind the door went down at an almost perfect forty-five-degree angle, leaving no room beyond the door for anything but a set of descending stairs.

The smaller building was like the guard station they had passed on their way in. It was older, ramshackle, and unused for many years. Sand

and sun had worn down the wood, and the window was broken out.

"There was a fence here once," Ventura pointed out when they were close enough.

Stumps of the steel fenceposts were still in the sand, mostly buried. Ventura used his hand to uncover them. The metal had been melted away, long ago from the looks of things.

One side of the guard station was scorched black, with the wood nearly carbonized. Dust had settled into the pocked holes, and it was brittle and flaked away under Shane's touch, leaving his fingers stained black.

"Not quite the welcome mat, but not a 'go away', either." Coulson took hold of the heavy, red door set into the concrete wall. It was pushed over but not closed. If the Burnt Soul had been last to leave, he'd left it open for anyone else to head down.

"I'd call that a 'go away'." Ventura pointed to Coulson's feet.

Shane looked at where Ventura was pointing but said nothing. The breeze blew sand across an exposed skull of a charred skeleton, collapsed just feet from the door.

CHAPTER 8

BEHIND THE RED DOOR

Three skeletons were in the sand next to the concrete bunker. One had collapsed in front of the door, and the other two were slightly farther away. Two had weapons on them, what had once been automatic rifles. The extreme heat had softened and wilted the barrels.

"It all looks old," Ventura said. "Years. Decades even."

"Our timeline is pretty open," Shane agreed.

The skeletons could have been two years old or seventy. The fact that no one had moved them was telling. Either no one had come back in all that time, or no one had been there long enough to do any housekeeping.

"Do you think any of this stuff is radioactive? Guess we should've brought the Geiger counters." Ventura stopped himself from touching one of the guns. "Are we at risk?"

"More or less risk than tracking ghosts that can melt sand?" Shane asked.

"At least I can see those things coming," Ventura said. "Radiation is not something I know how to deal with."

"Doc said it was controlled," Coulson said. "The area out here was safe enough. They worked in these labs for years. I think the only danger is if one of them comes after us."

"One did," Ventura reminded him.

"I took as much of that as I could," Coulson said casually, pushing the skeleton at the bunker door aside with his foot.

"You can absorb radiation?" the agent asked.

"Being dead has its perks. Not many, but some," Coulson confirmed.

"It was… hard."

Ventura glanced at Shane but did not comment. The worry was plain on his face. He was keen to put an end to dangerous ghosts and Shane didn't doubt his commitment, but Coulson also didn't take on suicide missions. He knew when he was outmatched.

"Let's see where Sparky was hiding out." Shane nodded to the door. "Keep your eyes and ears open, and if we need to, we fall back and regroup. It's more than a mile back to the fence line, so we know these Burnt Souls aren't escaping and can't pose a risk to anyone out in the world. We can figure out a better plan of attack if it comes to that."

It was sound advice to fall back in the face of a superior enemy until a new plan could be devised, but Shane wasn't confident that everyone else in Nevada was safe. If people like Bennet Ross and others were actively removing the dead from inside the restricted areas, someone could get their hands on one of the Burnt Souls. If a lead box containing one was opened in the heart of Las Vegas, tens of thousands of people could die. If they were dropped in a place like New York or L.A., with no one capable of stopping them or even understanding what was happening, that number could reach hundreds of thousands or more.

"Maybe we need to be more proactive before we rush down those stairs into God knows what," Ventura suggested. "These are walking nuclear weapons. This is serious, and we need people who can handle this. Work out the details later. If someone wants to cover it up, so be it. But that can happen after. We need to worry about saving lives now, not when it's too late."

The FBI agent in Xander Ventura always wanted to err on the side of caution. Shane couldn't fault him for the sentiment; Ventura was trying to do the right thing. But he was still too wrapped up in the idea of what he thought the right thing was, and of what the safe choices were. That was not how things worked.

"Who would we call?" Coulson asked. "This is not a government job."

"We don't need to say 'ghosts'," Ventura said. "The haunted items are irradiated. We just busted Ross in Las Vegas; this is an extension of that case. We have all the makings of a terrorist threat here. The FBI is equipped to respond to this. We can expose this lab and this restricted area and put a stop to whoever is running these experiments before containment gets breached further."

"I like where your head's at, kid. I do," Coulson said, "but what happens when your team runs in here and someone opens one of those boxes? This triangle of desert we're in doesn't officially exist. This is an uncharted, unclaimed, unknown piece of land that's home to some of the most dangerous stuff I've ever heard of. Imagine the resources behind this, Agent Ventura. Who's running PULSE 2? Who can conduct experiments on the dead for over fifty years without a whisper of it reaching the real world? If you think whoever is doing this is above making an entire team of FBI agents disappear and filing paperwork to say they all died of Havana syndrome, you're not paying attention."

"This is a coverup," Ventura said adamantly. "You shine light in the shadows, and it exposes them."

"Then you've never faced a shadow that fought back and swallowed the light," Coulson countered.

Shane clapped a hand on Ventura's shoulder.

"If we keep the numbers small, fewer people have to die," he said. "And I don't plan on dying."

"Easy for you guys to say," Ventura lamented. "He's already dead, and you're a Ghostbuster. I'm a guy with a metal stick."

"Keep that stick handy, Mulder. I'll get you through this alive," Coulson said. He opened the red door and disturbed more of the sand. The door stuck when it was nearly fully open, the corner catching on an object in the shadow of the concrete frame.

"It's a box." Shane bent to look at it.

It had once been a lead-lined wooden box, older and plainer than the kind he was used to seeing. It had a more utilitarian look to it, but there was no doubt it housed a haunted item. Remnants of it remained.

The box was mostly destroyed, broken to pieces and scorched. The lead inside had melted and warped like taffy. The wood was burned black in some places and reduced to splinters in others.

There were fragments in the box, unrecognizable to anyone who didn't already know what they were looking at. But Shane did. They were burned and broken fragments of bone. A human skull, and some other bits. The Burnt Soul's remains had been in the box, destroyed when Shane destroyed the ghost linked to them.

"It was just sitting out here," he said.

The box had to have been open in the sand. That explained the three corpses nearby, probably the unlucky ones who were there when the box was opened. But if it happened years ago, then one of them had opened the box, intentionally or accidentally, and that had been the end of it. The box fell, the men died, and the Burnt Soul had wandered ever since.

Shane assumed it had come from the bunker, and maybe, it had accessed the building after its release. But it was not from there. It was a wandering soul. Truly, then, no one had been to the bunker since its release. No one had imprisoned the ghost or laid its victims to rest. No one had cared for decades.

"I don't understand how the PULSE lab is still running if no one has been to this place since this ghost was released. What's down there?" Shane asked.

"Let's go look." Coulson stood at the threshold of the red door and looked into the waiting darkness.

The dead man led the way down, his feet making no sound on the stairs. Shane and Ventura's footsteps clanked on the metal, making a quiet approach impossible.

Ventura had a flashlight at the ready and cast the light down. The steps and walls were coated in dust, as was the rickety handrail bolted into one concrete wall. Some of the bolts had come loose over time, and the railing wobbled when Ventura put weight on it.

By the time they reached the bottom and the tiny square of concrete that awaited them, they were maybe thirty or forty feet below ground. The stairs came to a stop at another red metal door. The heavy latch was unbolted so that the door was closed but not sealed.

There were no sounds in the darkness. Coulson raised a hand but said nothing before walking through the closed door rather than opening it. Shane waited next to Ventura until Coulson returned seconds later.

"Hallway," Coulson whispered. "Four doors. Nothing alive that I saw. Powered down and layered in dust. It's as dead as aboveground."

"Any Burnt Souls?" Shane asked.

Coulson shrugged.

"No one popped out to say hello, but I didn't bang a drum to sound my arrival, either."

"Let's take a look." Shane grabbed the door handle.

The door was heavier than it looked, but the hinges made little noise beyond a soft grinding sound caused by trapped dust. The air was stale and old, not as dry as aboveground but by no means humid. It was cooler, though, and carried the faint hint of something burnt.

Coulson raised his hand as they entered the hall, producing a flame above his fingers like a torch. It illuminated much of the hallway but there was little to see beyond dust, doors, and concrete.

"7 A." Ventura stopped at the first door and read what was painted in white over the red. The next door was 7 B, and so on down to the final door, 7 D.

7 A was unlocked. Ventura lifted the handle and pushed the door in, flooding the interior with light as he entered. The room was small, set up with two sofas and two lounge chairs as well as a table and a small kitchenette. There was a record player on a shelf with some albums, books, and board games.

A Stratego board, still set up with its little dusty red and blue game pieces, was on the table and midgame. Open cans of beer, long since drunk or evaporated, sat next to the board along with a half-eaten Clark bar.

"Break room," Shane guessed, opening the refrigerator and wincing at the interior. Some items had molded and dehydrated ages earlier, but there were still a dozen cans of Coors on a shelf and some ancient condiments.

"Not living up to what I had built up in my mind." Ventura swept the bookshelf with his flashlight.

The record collection was a mix of rock, blues, jazz, and a few classical albums. The books ranged from works on physics to pulp horror to a handful of comic books.

"You have to be kidding me," Ventura said louder than any of them had spoken since they got down there.

"What?" Shane asked.

Ventura held up a comic book.

"Do you know what this is? Marvel Spotlight issue five. This is the first appearance of Ghost Rider."

Coulson's torch dimmed, and he looked at Shane.

"You brought this guy?" he said.

"This is worth a quarter of a million dollars," Ventura said.

Shane barked a laugh and shook his head.

"We'll come back for it after. You can add it to your collection," he said.

"They have the first Adam Warlock here, too!"

Ventura's excitement was blunted by the sound of grinding hinges in the hallway. He dropped the stack of comics and pulled out his iron baton.

Coulson's torch winked out as Shane pressed his back to the concrete wall next to the exit. Someone had opened one of the other doors in the hallway.

They were not alone in the bunker.

Chapter 9
BUNKER 7

Ventura took cover behind one of the sofas, leaving the flashlight on the bookshelf, its beam pointed at the exit. Coulson moved behind the door without sound. Shane was the only one who would be seen, but only once whoever was outside entered the room. He breathed slowly and evenly, forcing calm on himself even as his hands balled into fists, ready to strike.

The door to the breakroom shifted. Nothing had touched it, but Shane felt a gentle burst of cold air wash over him.

A second burst of air pushed the door open more, faintly grinding the hinges until a figure appeared in the doorway in the glow of the flashlight's beam. It moved slowly, carefully, and soundlessly.

Flesh sagged from the face of what had once been a man. It reminded Shane of Doc, only with much more grievous wounds. The flesh across the ghost's body hung like it was the thinnest membrane, bulging with fluid. The ghost was swollen with blisters like water balloons, seeping and oozing onto the floor from its pores.

It quivered as it moved, the fluid threatening to burst from the endless, strained sacks of skin. It smelled pungent and sour like vinegar or spoiled wine. It burned Shane's eyes and made them water, but he didn't move as the slow-moving thing sloshed its ungainly frame forward.

Eyes hidden deep within the swollen, blistered eyelids searched the room. They caught the light, reflecting it with a wet glimmer. It turned its body toward Shane, and he saw it bulging at odd angles all over. There was little definition left that indicated a human shape. The neck had swollen massively on one side, a blister the size of a grapefruit causing it to bend its neck sharply away from it.

There were no clothes on the ghost. Either they'd been burned off or the ghost had just returned without them for some reason. Shane couldn't imagine any garments fitting its irregular, warped form, anyway.

Its eyes fell on Shane and widened. The chasm of a mouth, tucked beneath a sagging, translucent lip, dropped open, and the ghost produced a rattling sound. Shane was on it swiftly. It was not one of the Burnt Souls, so any danger of the scorching attack was not a consideration.

Shane grabbed the ghost about the throat. The blisters on its neck and upper chest burst, gushing a syrupy fluid across his hand and up his forearm. His eyes watered as the smell strengthened.

Shane punched the spirit in the face with his other hand, forcing it back into the hall. The eye blisters exploded and sprayed him with more sticky, foul-smelling liquid before the ghost stumbled and fell onto the floor.

Head-to-toe back blisters burst, and the floor was coated in yellow-brown sludge that washed over Shane's boots. The ghost howled and Shane was forced to turn away as the fumes from the fluid burned his eyes.

He turned back into the room, shaking his head, and squeezing his eyes shut.

Coulson was out from behind the door, moving in a blur as Shane blinked away the burning.

"Ease up on it," Coulson said from the hallway. "Unless you want to lose some limbs."

The smell subsided, and the remnants on Shane's skin melted away. Ventura was on his feet, covering his nose with his arm and holding the flashlight on the doorway, Coulson was situated in the center of the light's beam, standing over the blistered ghost with one foot on its chest.

"I never hurt you," the ghost on the ground lamented. "I never attacked anyone."

Shane stepped back into the hall, his eyes watering and nose running.

The pungent acidity of the fluid had vanished, but his body was still dealing with the effects.

The ghost stared at them all, trapped under Coulson's foot but not fighting to escape. Its loose flesh, hanging in limp twists and flaps where the blisters had broken, made it look pathetic.

"Who are you?" Shane asked.

"Edward Walsh," the ghost answered. "Eddie. I work here. *Worked* here. Live here, maybe."

Eddie was hoarse, but he spoke quickly and desperately like he feared he was being mugged.

"What did you do here?" Shane continued.

"I worked in the lab. I helped prepare the Burners. Blood samples, vitals, and stress tests. I got them lunch," he explained.

"Eddie the lunch guy," Shane said.

Eddie groaned and nodded, his hands up in a placating manner despite still being laid out on the floor.

"I could have done more. Dr. Burroughs ran the lab, and I confirmed the numbers. I never hurt anyone. I stay here. I keep hidden. I didn't do anything."

"What's a Burner?" Ventura interrupted the ghost before he could say more.

Eddie looked at him and Coulson carefully removed his foot, letting the ghost scramble back to the far wall and sit up.

"Burners. From the main lab. Post-biologicals. They burned."

"The Burnt Souls," Ventura said. "Like our friend in Doomtown."

Eddie shook his head, the effort threatening to burst the massive neck blister.

"Not the Burnt Souls. Burners. Burnt souls were the first phase. Burners were the second phase."

"Second phase of what?" Coulson asked.

"Second phase of the Phoenix Project," Eddie said as if that explained things.

Shane crouched to look Eddie in the eye. The smell was there again, so close to the ghost, but it was bearable.

"Pretend we have no idea what you're talking about. Who runs this project? What's it for? And where are the Burners?"

Eddie shook his head, threatening to burst his neck blister again.

"Phoenix Project runs Phoenix Project. It's a think tank. Military, scientific, and governmental. We're making soldiers. Protecting America. We're doing this to save the world."

Shane sighed and nodded.

"Radioactive ghosts but patriotic. Got it."

"No," Eddie said. "No, no, no. Burnt souls are the radioactive ones. Phase One only. The Burners burn clean. They burn clean! That was the point."

"What do you mean by 'clean'?"

"The energy. The energy in the post-biologics is infinitely mutable. You force them from the biological body at the right concentration and bombard the remains until the post-biological returns, and you get a Burner. Cold burn. Negative stimulation return until reaction is achieved. Energy that has the properties of gamma radiation but no signature. Not radioactive. No side effects, no danger. Untraceable. The perfect soldier."

Shane looked at Ventura and then Coulson. A haze of smoke hung about Coulson's head, and he took the phantom cigarette from between his lips.

"This guy's brain is a little soft. I'm not sure what the hell he means."

"I'll show you. I'll show you!" Eddie got awkwardly to his feet.

Shane took a step back, and the ghost pointed down the hall to the door marked 7 D.

"That's the lab. I'll show you. Come on."

He hobbled down the hallway, fearful of being attacked again. Coulson stayed close, illuminating the path with his torch, and Shane and

Ventura followed behind.

The door to 7 D was open, and inside was a sprawling lab space with several desks and ancient computer equipment that was as bulky as it was dusty. Reel-to-reel machines the size of refrigerators covered an entire wall, and a panel with dozens of switches, buttons, and a handful of thin microphones was set before a window that overlooked a room recessed into the earth.

Shane peered over the control panel at the room on the other side of the window. Some kind of metallic pillar set into the wall stretched up into the ceiling, and a series of metal rods protruded from the floor and walls around a small, empty square in the center of the room.

"What is this?" he asked.

"That's it. That's the Burn Room," Eddie said.

The ghost leaned forward and tapped on the glass.

"Lead shielded. Safe for us. Subjects waited there." He pointed to the empty square. "We monitor up here. Bombard them with radiation from the pillar."

"These were living subjects? Volunteers?" Shane asked.

"Soldiers." Eddie nodded. "It was… difficult. We turned off the speakers. The screaming was long. Painful. If the post-biological separates, we start the negative stimulation here."

He showed Shane a series of buttons across several panels in a grid formation, numbered sequentially.

"What is this?"

"Iron. Iron stimulates post-biologicals. The mechanism is not understood. Atomic structure interacting and interfering with energy waves? Unclear." Eddie shook his head as though frustrated.

"These buttons correspond to those rods in the room?"

"Negative stimulation. Continual bombardment on volunteer until a reaction occurs. Or doesn't."

Shane looked at Coulson, who stared down into the room.

"So, you killed a volunteer, and if his ghost appeared, you poked him with iron rods again and again, forcing him back to his remains or whatever haunted item he had until he lost his marbles and went nuclear?"

He turned back to Eddie, and the ghost's eyes darted nervously from Coulson to Shane and Ventura and back.

"Oh. Um. It's more complicated than that."

"But that's it, right? You just irradiated and tortured this ghost until it displayed some kind of defense mechanism. A better version of the Burnt Souls?"

"Yes." Eddie nodded.

"How long did it take?" Ventura asked.

"Results were never typical. Our fastest success was, um… five days. Well, one hundred and fourteen hours."

"And where are your successes now, Eddie?" Shane asked.

The ghost was silent for a moment, looking into Shane's eyes. The blisters on his face seemed to pulse, and the beads of fluid grew fat and then trickled down, dripping from his cheeks to his chest.

"There was a breach," he said softly.

The ghost turned his head and looked at something on the far side of the room, in the shadows beyond the light of Coulson's torch. Ventura pointed his flashlight. In the corner of the room, pressed against one of the ancient computer terminals, was a jumble of human remains. Shane counted at least four people based on the skulls, but it could have been more. The bodies were badly burnt, almost ash in the center with just bits around the outside having been burned black. The computer and the floor were barely burned.

"How many escaped?" Shane asked.

"Just one," Eddie answered. "The others were always moved. Never more than two at a time in any bunker. We were transferring. New acquisition from Bunker 9. I don't know what happened."

"So this was done by one of your Burners," Ventura said. "They can control their power this precisely? Burn a body but not the walls around it?"

"They can burn you inside out," Eddie said. "Perfect control. The Burnt Souls are on or off. No precision. But a Burner like Arkady can do what she wants."

"Arkady?" Coulson asked.

"Oh. Um, Lieutenant Joanne Arkady. She did this. She killed me."

"And she's out there loose in the desert?" Ventura asked. He looked through the window again, at the empty room where they ran their experiments. "Where's her body? Her haunted item?"

"Don't know." Eddie shrugged apologetically. "It was gone when I, you know, came back."

"What year was it when you died, Eddie?" Shane asked.

"Has it been years? I mean, it has. Must have been. I've been here a long time, haven't I?"

"What year?" Shane asked again.

"Nineteen seventy-three. Is it... what year is it now?"

Ventura looked away awkwardly, and Shane sighed.

"When's the last time you left the bunker?"

"Never left. Not like this. I can't... I wouldn't want to be in the light. Not like this."

He indicated his appearance, gesturing in a clumsy manner at his seeping blisters and refusing to maintain eye contact.

"Do you want to know how long it's been?" Shane asked.

He did not have any need to keep the truth a secret from the ghost, but he knew that it would be hard to learn the truth that more than half a century had passed.

"It's been a long time." Eddie nodded. "Maybe... maybe not. Maybe I don't need to know."

Chapter 10
Trapped

"Tell me about Lieutenant Arkady," Coulson said. "What can she do aside from spot cremations? Is she coherent? Rational?"

Eddie had settled into a spot near his remains, crouched like he was huddled for warmth. His blisters oozed liquid that pooled around where he sat.

"I don't know," the ghost answered.

"What do you mean you don't know? Wasn't the point of the experiment to study her?"

"To study the control function demonstrated by a Phase Two Burner," Eddie replied. "To elicit a response and make the subject exercise controlled usage."

"Did you ever ask her if she could do what you needed her to do?" Coulson asked.

Eddie looked confused for a moment and then shook his head.

"We… no. It was not a self-reporting procedure. Subject feedback was not deemed necessary."

"Jesus." Coulson shook his head as another cigarette appeared in his mouth. "Are you telling me that you beat that ghost with iron rods for hours and hours to make her do something you didn't even ask her to do in the first place? Don't you think that would have saved time?"

"No," the ghost replied. "I mean, it never came up."

"What *did* come up?" Shane redirected the conversation. "You improved on the Burnt Soul, and you created a weapon that can focus radiation? Is that it?"

"We completed Phase Two. The Burners have precision and control. But, you know, we never controlled them. That was a problem. Lead was the only control method we had. Lead-lined rooms or containers. But there was an incident on the night of the breach, and we lost containment. I don't know how the other bunkers fared."

"How many phases are there, Eddie?" Shane asked.

"I don't know. Phase Three was not my job. I never asked."

Shane looked at his companions but said nothing. The Burnt Souls were dangerous enough on their own, and the Burners were an upgrade. If Phase Three was launched in the lab or one of the other bunkers in the desert, he couldn't imagine how the danger had increased, but it must have been. The goal seemed to be the most dangerous ghost they could produce.

"I know one thing," Eddie said. "One aspect we counted as a failure, a holdover from Phase One, was range. The post-biologicals have a range limit, a seemingly arbitrary distance from root. We calculated it at approximately one mile. Every subject was the same with a variance of no more than two percent. I always assumed Phase Three would improve upon that."

"So, Arkady is still probably within the one-mile radius," Coulson said. "Assuming her haunted item is around somewhere."

"The bunkers were built a mile and a half apart to ensure safer operation. But in the event of a containment breach, emergency protocols were implemented. That was why the bunkers were built here, in the no-man's land beyond the Yucca Flat. In the event of loss of containment, the bunkers were to be sacrificed. No one in or out. Ever," Eddie said.

Shane grunted. The dead bodies at the door in the desert made sense. The bunker had been abandoned. They knew the ghosts could not travel more than a mile, so they set up a containment of more than a mile and just forgot about them.

"What if you had lived? Or the others in the other bunkers? Someone must have survived," Ventura said.

"Containment protocol was very clear," Eddie replied. "Nothing is allowed to reach the fence. They called it the Burn Zone. A triangle of space on the map. If it's still standing, the guards have orders to kill on sight. If the Burners don't get you first, I suppose."

Eddie had nothing else to share about the other bunkers or the PULSE lab. He had worked in Bunker 7 and nowhere else. He knew nothing about any other work being done or whether the other bunkers fell when his did.

The stale air seemed heavier after their conversation, and Shane had no interest in talking to the ghost any longer. He left him there, crouched by his half-ashen body, and headed back up the stairs into the daylight.

Shane winced in the sunlight when he was back topside. The heat was as bad as ever, but it still felt more refreshing than the bunker. The warm breeze smelled cleaner and was less oppressive.

"So, we walked into a minefield like idiots." Ventura joined him outside. "This is why you don't cross fences that say 'no trespassing'. There's a reason former nuclear testing sites are dangerous."

"You don't say?" Shane took a cigarette from his pack and lit it.

Coulson joined them a second later, unfazed by the sunlight or change in temperature.

"Not as helpful as it could have been," he said.

"I don't know. I like knowing there are two kinds of radioactive ghosts that might kill me," Ventura said. "We need to get out of here."

"I don't know if getting shot is better than being burned, but I'm already dead, so what do I know?" Coulson said.

"I don't want to experience either," Ventura said. "Can't you Jedi Mind Trick them again so we can get back to town and maybe come at this thing in a less suicidal way?"

Coulson took a long drag on his phantom cigarette, squinting for no good reason and nodding slowly before he took the smoke from his lips with two fingers and used it to point at Ventura.

"Funny you should ask," he said.

"Why is that funny?" Ventura asked seriously.

"The guards didn't have standing orders to shoot people on the way in. I got close enough to talk to them and influence what they were thinking. But coming from this side of the fence, they're going to shoot before we get close. There's no way I can get in range before they take shots at you two."

Ventura pulled his lower lip into his mouth, chewing on it as he shook his head, staring at Coulson.

"Then how were we going to get out of here?"

"Hadn't planned that far ahead," the ghost admitted.

Ventura turned to Shane, a fire building in his eyes.

"I'm here because I trust you, Ryan. Because I thought we'd be putting an end to someone trafficking in dangerous ghosts. What the hell are we doing now?"

Shane exhaled smoke. He was annoyed at Coulson as well but hadn't expected him to be so brazenly glib about his lack of planning. It seemed unlike him, at least in terms of their limited time together. Coulson was generally nothing if not well-prepared. The man could see what others were thinking, and it made him a formidable force.

"You've been lying," he said to Coulson.

"I've been known to bend the truth," the ghost replied.

Shane shook his head and removed his cigarette.

"You're worse off than you let on. You can't plan ahead because you lost the ability. How screwed are we, Coulson?"

The ghost's expression was grim, but he allowed himself a humorless smile.

"The Burnt Soul almost tapped me. I don't know what happened but I'm... I'm mostly just me now. Got a few parlor tricks—cigarettes and light bulbs—but I can't even touch your mind right now. I can't sense anything, people or ghosts. Anywhere."

"So what happens if you take on another one?" Shane asked.

Coulson dropped his cigarette in the sand, and it fizzled from existence.

"You're gonna have to finish that fight for me, I think," he answered.

Shane hadn't joined up with Coulson expecting the ghost to handle his fights for him. He never expected anyone to do that. But he'd be a fool if he hadn't planned to use Coulson for his abilities when they were needed. And fighting ghosts that could burn them to ash in seconds was something they needed Coulson for.

The idea of Coulson being vulnerable was a wrinkle they needed to iron out quickly. He was on equal footing with Shane and Ventura now. He would be destroyed if they were caught off-guard again. It didn't mean they were finished, it just meant a clear shift in strategy.

"We're not dead yet," Shane said. "Eddie said there are other bunkers. Some might have lost containment or maybe not. Maybe that means others have more information, something else we can use. A mile and a half to the next one. Let's assume Bunker 8 is north and Bunker Six is south."

"Eight is great." Coulson headed off without waiting to see if the others agreed.

Shane pinched out his cigarette and stashed the butt before following the ghost with Ventura at his side.

"He's going to get us killed," Ventura said as they walked.

"He's going to get himself killed," Shane corrected. "If we go, it'll be on us."

"You believe that?"

"He was willing to move Heaven and Earth to save a woman named Jillian when I met him. He was doing the bidding of the Cult of the Endless Night so they'd let her live. He walked into my house like he owned the place and kidnapped Carl but didn't hurt anyone. He stole ghosts right out of my damn hands but didn't kill me when he could have, or when they told him to. And then later, he helped me set off a nuclear weapon in a mountain to put an end to the cult for good. Thomas Coulson scares me and not much does, but he does not half-ass things. If he thinks he's not going to survive this, I trust him. He'll go up in flames to get this job done," Shane said.

"But he's a ghost," Ventura said. "How can he die?"

"He's his own haunted item. The Burnt Souls and the radiation here are tapping his reserves. Sounds like the whole thing is going to fall apart, and if he's not rooted to a real thing, like his remains or a dagger, a coin, whatever you please, he's gone."

Ventura exhaled loudly as they trudged across the sand. Coulson left no footprints and was not slowed by the ungainly trek. He was getting farther and farther ahead of the other two.

"I get that you're used to life-and-death stuff, so maybe this isn't as apocalyptic to you as it is to me, but I still don't see a way out of this for us," Ventura said after a moment.

"Worst-case scenario, you call in your team from Las Vegas and we have to explain why we're in a restricted area," Shane suggested.

Ventura laughed. He reached into his pocket and pulled out his phone.

"That'd be a great idea, except my phone is dead. Happened after the ghost blazed up on us in Doomtown. Think it fried the processor."

"Well, then we've got about a half-mile of walking left to consider a Plan B," Shane said.

He was aware of the risks Ventura was worried about, but they were in the thick of it now, and their best bet as far as Shane could see was to proceed. The guards had orders to shoot on sight, but someone was getting around that fence with irradiated ghosts. Some of the Burnt Souls or Burners might have already been taken. Someone was complicit, and that, in Shane's eyes, meant something in Eddie's Burn Zone was still active.

The bunkers might have all been decommissioned in the seventies, but there were still some secrets to be uncovered. And there was still a chance that Shane could take out the ghosts without having to rely on Coulson, if he was fast enough.

As worried as Ventura was, Shane was not there yet. They would have to face something worse than what they'd already seen before he was willing to pack it in.

CHAPTER 11

THE BURN ZONE

Bunker 8 was nearly identical to Bunker 7. Where 7 had been damaged by an irradiated ghost, 8 was pristine. The guard station shack was in one piece; it was just empty.

No corpses marred the sands around the red door that led into Bunker 8. Unlike 7, the door here was sealed, and it looked for all the world like the place had never been used. Only the wear and tear of years of sun and sand spoke to its age.

Shane tried the door handle, and it was seized up tight. There was a brief, barely noticeable shift before it stopped, and resisted his attempts to move it further. He tried it from several angles to change his leverage, but it refused to budge.

Ventura tried to aid Shane in moving the long, lever-like handle, forcing his weight against it, but it resisted.

"Let me see what I can do." Coulson approached the door and leaned in to inspect it.

"You sure?" Ventura asked. "I don't want you wasting whatever juice you have on a door."

"I assure you I have the juice, Agent Ventura," Coulson said. "Besides, this one is physics. Scorching day, metal door, things expand."

The ghost inserted his hand into the door and waved it back and forth like he was making ripples in water. The natural cold given off by a ghost was not something Coulson usually displayed, but it must have been well within his power. The metal whined softly, and Shane grabbed the handle again, pressing and pulling at the same time.

The door handle moved, slowly at first but then more easily. In seconds, the grinding hinges were moving as the door pulled open. Shane had only opened it a crack when a screaming klaxon alarm went off on the inside.

Shane released the handle as the alarm wailed, screeching over and again with a piercing, abrasive sound that cut through his skull.

"This day keeps getting better," Ventura shouted, covering his ears.

Coulson was half-immersed in the door, climbing it from the inside like a ladder until he reached high enough inside the concrete structure to force his hand inside the alarm and cut it off at the source.

The sound died, but only outside. A second alarm was still going somewhere down in Bunker 8. Shane was about to suggest just closing the door and forgetting about it when a shift in the desert breeze caught his attention. There was another alarm.

"Coulson, can you—" Ventura began. He cut himself off when Shane raised a hand.

Shane's head was up, focused on nothing with his eyes but relying on his ears. He turned in a half-circle in the soft sand. The klaxon sounded in the northeast and south. He could hear it repeating and overlapping. More than two. Some were faint and more distant.

"They're all going off," Shane said. "We set them all off."

"But no one's here, right? That's what Eddie said. These were abandoned decades ago," Ventura said.

"No one living," Coulson added.

The ghost pushed the door shut and lifted the handle to reseal it. The alarms kept going, but a new sound joined them. A rumbling, deep and mechanical. And it was growing closer.

"What the hell is that?" Ventura backed away quickly.

The sand around Shane's feet vibrated, flowed, and wobbled like it was liquid, covering a wide swath of desert in front of the bunker door.

The rumbling grew louder like an engine coming closer. With it, the vibrations grew stronger. Shane backed away in one direction and Ventura moved in another, escaping the patch of quaking sand. Coulson stayed at the bunker doors.

Gears rattled, and something erupted from the sand. Metal doors rose from the earth and spread like a blooming, steel flower, erecting a simple, square frame in the space Shane had just stood. A cargo elevator rumbled up from below, just a simple metal platform held in the frame by steel cables.

In the center of the platform, three charred, black skeletons shook and swayed as the elevator came to a stop. Each was black as soot and had no living tissue left on it, and they all moved slowly as though the elevator had just roused them from a deep slumber.

There was no glow, no burning, or any sound after the elevator stopped, but there didn't need to be. Shane knew already what they were.

"Ventura, move your ass!" he shouted.

He was running across the sand before the words were out of his mouth. The closest of the skeletons shifted and swayed toward the sound of his voice. No eyes filled those empty sockets, only the blackness inside an empty skull, but it began to glow with a soft, white light as soon as it faced him.

Shane was on the elevator platform in seconds. He grabbed the skeleton by the skull and twisted it as he jumped and spun his body around, holding it tightly so it was forced to spin and fall to the ground with him. They landed hard, and the ghost's vertebrae snapped cleanly. The blast was not as powerful as the first Burnt Soul had been, but it still knocked Shane from the elevator, sending him skidding back into the sand.

The force of the first ghost's destruction was enough to knock over the other two, both of whom had already started to glow.

Ventura had reached the ghosts and brought down one of his iron batons toward the spirit's glowing skull. The ghost caught him by the wrist before the blow landed, and he screamed. Shane saw smoke rising from the man's flesh.

The Burnt Soul reached for the iron baton, and Ventura released his grip as the metal glowed red. Coulson's hand on the ghost's wrist was all that saved Ventura from bursting into flames as he pried it back.

"Get to cover." Coulson jerked the glowing spirit away from Ventura and pushed it off the elevator into the sand.

The third spirit was already glowing too brightly to look at. Shane kept his eyes averted, turning his back on it as he pulled Ventura away and headed for the guard station.

Coulson swung at the only spirit still standing, but his efforts counted for little. The sound of rumbling fire grew, filling the silence, and the heat coming from the spirit increased by the second.

"You two better hurry," Coulson shouted over the growing roar.

Shane kicked in the door of the guard station and fell to the floor, and Ventura came in after him. He pushed the door shut as Ventura removed his jacket, pulling it over their heads as the searing light from the Burnt Souls flooded the guard station's tiny window.

"We're in a wooden shack." Ventura laughed inexplicably as he turned his head to face the floor. "We're going to die as mesquite barbecue."

"This is cheap pine," Shane said.

There was a pause, and then Ventura laughed again as the station shook. Shane smelled the smoke and felt the heat. If he could have picked any way to die, burning to death would not have been it. But most people didn't get to choose.

"Ryan, I want you to know you've made my life absolutely chaotic, but I've never felt more like I had a reason to be here than I have since I met you. I'm glad to be dying with you," Ventura said.

"Really? I don't want to die at all," Shane replied.

Ventura laughed again, and Shane joined him. He could think of worse people to die with than Xander Ventura.

The guard station shook violently as a sound like a pair of jets battered the walls. The wooden planks were torn apart in a gust of scorching hot air, and then... nothing.

The light vanished, and Shane pushed Ventura's jacket away. The guard station had collapsed. The two Burnt Souls were still standing, but they were black skeletons again.

"What happened?" Ventura asked.

The ghosts were taking slow, shaky steps toward them. Coulson emerged from the concrete wall of the bunker and waved his arm in a furious warning to flee.

"They're charging for Round Two," he yelled. "Go!"

Shane pulled Ventura to his feet and ran, heading east this time toward a small mountain range. The skeletons were slowly building up a new glow, but it was not as fast this time. Their energy was not unlimited, or at least not rapid-fire.

Coulson joined Ventura and Shane, striding above the sand without touching it. In the distance to the northeast and farther south, Shane watched pillars of light rise from the horizon like blasts of white fire. Some were single, and some were in clusters of three, but he knew what each of them was. The Burnt Souls were firing off at random.

"They're just exploding," Ventura said. "All of them."

They had to be the Phase One experiments. Powerful but not ideal at all. They were almost like animals. Not even. Animals understood how to attack and defend. This was more like a Venus Flytrap. Any kind of stimulation, and they'd go off.

"There are dozens." Ventura watched as more distant bursts of light went off.

Shane looked behind them. He could just make out the bunker, but the skeletons were nowhere to be seen. If they were still pursuing, they moved very slowly. Shane and the others would put a mile between them long before the skeletons had a chance to catch up.

"They're slow," he said. "Slow and stupid. Gives us another

advantage."

"As long as we have more shacks to hide in." Ventura tore a strip off his shirt to bandage the burn on his wrist.

They slowed their pace, but Shane shook his head.

"I took out that first one very easily. They're weak when they're not powered up. The experiments that made them broke them down badly. He practically fell apart in my hands. If I can better coordinate an attack, I can take out at least two next time."

"And if there are more?" Ventura asked.

"Then you need to be faster with the iron baton," Shane said.

Coulson had stopped ahead and was waiting for them to catch up. The sun was burning the top of Shane's head, adding to the minor burns he'd received from dealing with the Burnt Souls, and they had little water left. They needed to find a place to get out of the sun in the approaching rocky hills.

"There are caves up there," Coulson said once they caught up to him. Shane couldn't say whether the ghost had read his thoughts or had just been thinking the obvious.

"Any sign of ghosts?" Ventura asked.

"Still can't tell," Coulson answered. "More than a mile from the bunkers, though. We might be in the clear for now."

"Good enough," Ventura said.

Coulson matched pace with the two living men for the rest of the journey. The hills were farther away than Shane had imagined. He chalked it up to an optical illusion caused by the sun and the sand. By the time they climbed the rocky face, the sun was already descending for the evening. It looked as though they would be spending the night there.

The random lights that indicated the Burnt Souls were going off had become a rarer sight. Once the trio had climbed to a rocky plateau, the lights had stopped. Wherever the burned ghosts were, they were no longer trackable, even with the advantage of elevation in the hills.

Coulson left to explore a cave entrance while Shane and Ventura stayed outside looking back the way they had come. There was nothing to see, even though they were higher up. The desert stretched in every direction.

There were some mountains in the distance, but they had been in the distance from the start. There was no sign of the bunkers, the fence, or the town they had started from. It looked like they had walked to the end of the world.

Ventura passed Shane a water bottle, and he took a quick drink, just enough to remain hydrated. When they had looked at the map with Doc and Dezzy, the patch of land around Doomtown had not looked so large. Shane was fairly certain it was not as big as the desert grounds they had covered. They had gotten away from what was already charted and were somewhere else now. The problem was that he wasn't sure where that was. Nor was he sure where they should go next.

"Going to get cold once the sun is down." Shane headed for the cave entrance. "We should build a fire and make a plan for tomorrow."

"Yeah," Ventura said, staring out at the empty desert. "Let's do that."

CHAPTER 12
PULSE

The klaxon alarm continued uninterrupted. The repetitive, abrasive sound traveled across the desert, carrying on the occasional breeze to the ears of the few animals that lived in the Burn Zone.

A coyote lifted its head, ears upright and twisting toward the noise. It froze, smelled the air, and then ran in the opposite direction, its hackles raised.

Miles from the rocky hills, the alarm echoed from deep within the bowels of an unlabeled facility. Larger than any of the bunkers, the walls bore no markings to indicate who built it or what it was for. The only remarkable feature was the set of massive steel doors that had been melted to slag at the front entrance.

Once, long ago, the doors were painted red and required an electronic mechanism to activate gears and pulleys that would open them wide enough to allow Jeeps and trucks to enter. They were built to withstand heavy-arms fire and even explosions. Now, the steel looked like candle wax, lumped upon itself in bulbous, black piles to the left side of the entrance.

Sand caked in the crevices of the melted metal, and dust had taken some of the luster from it. The desert was never damp enough to form a rusty patina, but the metal had still oxidized and looked ancient and forgotten.

Past the melted door was a flat, metal platform large enough for two vehicles to park abreast. It was a freight elevator, but it had not been used in years. Next to it was a set of simple steel stairs that wound down alongside the elevator, serving as access for those on foot, or an emergency exit in the event of a power loss.

The alarm echoed up the stairs and the empty elevator shaft from below the ground. Unlike the bunkers, these steps continued deeper into the earth. The first floor was burned black with smoke and soot. Nothing was salvageable or even identifiable.

The stairs continued deeper past the second level, a third level, a fourth, and ultimately a fifth. The facility was much larger than it seemed from the outside. Laboratories, storage rooms, offices, and testing facilities filled the space on each level.

On the second floor, the abrasive alarm was answered by a scream in the dark. Lights flickered, and the shape of a skeleton blazed to life. The ghost leaned hard to one side, a fracture in its pelvic bone preventing it from standing straight. Every time the alarm rang out, a light born from the charred black bones pulsed as though fueled by the sound, growing brighter each time.

The skeleton screamed, and another answered it. They were aware of each other, at least in some rudimentary way, but they were not communicating. They cried out and their lights glowed brighter. One would eventually reach such a blinding brightness that the skeletal form could no longer hold the energy, and it would release in a fiery blast that spread like a ring throughout the facility, licking white-hot fire against the already burned walls.

The scene repeated itself on the third level. This time it was less dramatic and less powerful. Some of the spirits here still had flesh on their bones, though very little and not enough to identify who they might have been in life. They were ragged and burned like victims of a house fire, clinging to the last bits of what once made them human long ago.

Many more ghosts wandered the third floor than the second. Some could achieve the blinding glow of the Burnt Souls, but not most. They had not captured the power during the experimental phase. They had not been successes and were deemed failures, stored in the Level Three holding pen. They, too, screamed at the abrasive alarm.

At the bottom of the facility, on the lowest level where no fire had scorched the walls and no escaped experiments had ever scourged the flesh from the bones of their tormentors, a man lifted his head.

The alarm rang down the elevator shaft, but it sounded so distant to his ears. Had he not paused for a moment in his work, he might not have heard it. It was easy to get lost these days. To vanish into his work and forget about everything that happened above or that might be happening anywhere else. His world was underground in the dark, and he was happy to keep it that way. As happy as he could be anymore.

Weeks ago, the man had broken through the lab walls, tearing down solid stone, and cutting into the rock under the desert. He had a tunnel to dig. He had to get through the rock and find what was hidden down there.

There were days when he would find himself digging, sometimes with tools and sometimes with his bare hands like an animal. He would pause and struggle to remember what he was doing. Sometimes, he struggled to remember who he was. It was harder than it should have been. He realized as more time passed that it was becoming more common.

He used to talk to himself when he worked, just noise to keep himself company, but he was afraid to do so anymore. He was scared that if he talked to himself out loud, he would forget his name or forget the sound of his voice and not even know who he was talking to.

When he was alive, his mind had been his most valuable possession. He had never been hung up on material things, but his mind made him special. It was what made him important and what made other people seek him out. They wanted to know what he knew and wanted him to do things only he could do. So who was he if he no longer had his mind?

None of that mattered. He was getting distracted. The important thing was to keep digging the tunnel. He needed to break through the stone. No matter how long it took, he needed to keep going. That was his job now.

That would be his job forever if that was what it took. He was Plan B, and it was never wise to only have a Plan A.

His tunnel was long now, wide, and deep. He knew he had done good work. Physical labor was never his thing in life; he was not made for that. He was doing well now, but it still was not finished.

There were iron deposits in the rock, and he could not touch them. He had to use tools to get past them and be very careful as he did so. Iron was anathema to the dead like him. That was a thing they had learned in the experiments. Iron and lead. Post-biological entities did not respond positively to iron or lead.

It was strange being on the other side of it. Being one of them, a post-biological. A ghost. He could feel the iron now. He felt it repelling him, forcing him away at the slightest touch. There was no living sensation like it. The closest analogy he could think of was two magnets with an identical charge forcing each other away. He avoided it now. He knew better.

The ghost of the man returned to the tunnel entrance, hunched over and slow in his movements. His back was twisted, the spine showing through melted flesh where it had warped and mutated, the cells expanding and multiplying out of control before death had claimed him. It had left him in a hideous state of flux. He did not look completely human anymore. He was a monster. A creature born from his mistakes.

It had been one moment in the process of his death, one instant in which his cells divided too quickly after exposure to the non-biological radiation like a tumor run amok. But it had frozen his ghost in that moment, so he had to carry it with him eternally. Such a strange thing, but it didn't matter anymore. Nothing did.

Someone had accessed one of the bunkers. The alarm had not gone off in many years. He wasn't sure how many. He'd kept track for a while, tried to be analytical and observant. He'd tried to remain a scientist. But he had lost the will long ago. Decades was all he knew for sure.

No one was meant to access the bunkers again. Protocols were still in place. There was still order out there in the world, where people lived and worked and were ignorant of what happened in the desert.

He wasn't sure if it was anger or frustration that he felt more. It was not a good time for anyone to access the bunkers. It didn't even matter who it was. There was no scenario in which someone should have opened the door. There was no outcome that wouldn't lead to chaos. Maybe anger and frustration together.

The ghost heard the screams from the ones above him. He grumbled and moved across the lab, faster than a living being in his condition ever could have. His twisted body should have hobbled and barely been able to move. When he was alive, at the end, that was very much the case. He was not built to work properly any longer. He was ruined.

He reached a dusty control panel and pushed a button. The alarm stopped. The screams continued, and faint rumblings along with them. Bursts of energy. He had grown used to the sound over the years. The Burnt Souls were nothing if not predictable. They would rage and explode and rage again until finally they burned themselves out and wandered to a corner where they would stand as still as statues for another week, year, or decade. Until something disturbed them again.

A light sparked to life in the darkness. The ghost had been working in the dark for years. Light and dark no longer had control over what he saw or didn't see. The eyes of the dead saw everything. Nevertheless, the light grew brighter.

"Men have come," a voice in the light said.

The ghost grumbled, standing hunched to one side, and averting his eyes from the center of the blazing, white object. He was beyond pain now, but something in the light still irritated his senses.

"The Burnt Souls will kill them," the twisted ghost said.

"They don't matter. But they have tripped the test. There is no more containment."

The twisted spirit looked at the light, despite the discomfort.

"Anywhere?" he asked.

"Anywhere," the voice in the light confirmed.

The ghost groaned and shook his head. No containment anywhere. All the bunkers were open. His work was not done. He had not found the cell. Nothing was ready.

"You must finish," the voice in the light demanded.

"I am trying," he said.

He could go faster. He could be less wary of the iron deposits. The rock was full of it, but if he was cautious, he could still push on. There would eventually be a breakthrough. He would find the prison.

"There is no time, Yuri. Project Five will not wait, and the men above cannot discover it."

"Are they military?" Yuri asked. The military was not supposed to enter the Burn Zone. No one was.

"It doesn't matter, Yuri. They're here. Be swift."

"What if it is too late?" the ghost asked.

"Then I have enjoyed being your friend, Yuri," the voice answered. It was not what he expected, but it was also the only honest response he could have gotten.

The light winked out, and Yuri was alone in the dark again. Despite his assurances that he would try, it was impossible. He had been tunneling for weeks—since the others had come and released Project Five—and he had found nothing. Now, pressed and on a clock, he would have no more success in discovering the nest.

The men in the desert would die. The Burnt Souls would be harvested. Project Five would be free. All would be lost.

"And the world will end," Yuri muttered to himself.

CHAPTER 13

BY THE FIRELIGHT

Coulson sat cross-legged next to the fire opposite Shane. Ventura was laid out, using his folded-up jacket as a pillow, and they burned scraps of dried wood they had harvested from nearby scrub.

The ghost had found a pair of rabbits, which they roasted over the fire. Ventura had been reluctant to eat at first, refusing to believe they were in dire enough straits to have to hunt game, but he gave in once he smelled the meat over the open flame. They hadn't eaten since breakfast at the diner, and walking across the desert took a lot of energy.

"Are you feeling stronger?" Ventura asked, picking at the bones of his rabbit.

"Than what?" Coulson asked back.

"Than you were. Is it coming back to you?"

"No," the ghost answered. "It's like being trapped in a thick sweater and bulky gloves when you need precision movement in your arms and hands. Something about this place is limiting me."

"Think it'll be better if you leave?" Shane asked.

"You suggesting I go?" the ghost replied.

"If you're at risk of being destroyed out here, yes. You didn't come here expecting to put your life on the line."

"I already did that once," Coulson said, a cigarette appearing between his lips. "I died knowing what it meant and everything it entailed. I'd have to be a real jackass to back out of a job now, after I'm dead, for fear of the consequences."

"Did you do that before you two met?" Ventura asked.

"Do what?" Coulson asked.

"Chain smoke. You guys both chain smoke. Is that a thing ghost hunters do? Should I invest in a pipe?"

"I don't chain smoke," Shane said. "It's just regular heavy smoking."

"These aren't even real." Coulson flicked the cigarette at Ventura. It spun end over end and nearly hit the man, who scrambled back to avoid it before it faded from existence. A replacement was instantly back between Coulson's lips.

"John Constantine smoked all the time," Ventura said. "He hunted ghosts."

"Never met him," Coulson said.

"He's a comic book character," Ventura said. "It's just a thing everyone knows, I guess."

"Did the Ghostbusters smoke?" Coulson asked.

"Dan Aykroyd does in the movie," Shane confirmed. "Maybe Winston, too."

"Huh," Coulson said. "Maybe it *is* a thing everyone does. Except you, Ventura. I think this bodes poorly for you."

"Based on my current luck, maybe," Ventura agreed.

They watched the fire in silence for a while before Coulson started talking again.

"I've experienced radiation before. Had a job at a nuclear plant a while back. Plus that bomb we set off." He nodded at Shane. "This is different, though. Something out here is really keyed to ghosts. The experiments these bunkers were conducting did some weird stuff. I bet they didn't even realize half of what they were doing."

"Sounds like they were focused more on what they thought they knew than learning anything they didn't," Ventura added.

He wasn't wrong, Shane thought. Given what he had learned about ghosts in life, what he had learned from any outside source, he wasn't surprised. There was no "real" information about ghosts. Calling them post-biological entities didn't make them any more scientific and knowable. Those scientists were baking cakes without recipes and hoping everything turned out fine. Judging from the state of things he had seen so far, they were wrong.

"I want to know how Bennett Ross got in here," Shane said. "Guards with orders to shoot trespassers means he was let in. Burnt Souls blazing like the sun means he was either extremely lucky or knew how to avoid them."

"Maybe not," Coulson replied. "At least on that second point. The Burnt Souls are relatively new from what I have seen. I think it might have just been that one in Doomtown roaming free. Easy to miss."

"And the guards?" Shane asked.

"That's different. When I went to Doomtown the first time, that hole in the ground was only half dug up. From the surface, not below. Someone had been rooting around there, and it might have been your guy."

"Bennett Ross is a nobody," Ventura said. "A lowlife with a few connections out East who was making some money. How's he getting access to a place like this in any official capacity?"

"Who said it was official?" Coulson asked. "Those guards are probably local, right? Doesn't take much to line up the dominoes to get what you want around Las Vegas. He had money, they're guys just guarding a gate in the middle of nowhere. No reason to believe his presence here was sanctioned."

"This is stuff people get killed over," Ventura said.

"Fifty years ago," Coulson agreed. "Time has a way of tempering horror. Whoever is paying the salary of those guards probably doesn't know or care what's in these bunkers. Those guys probably don't even know there *are* bunkers. Some bigshot rolls up with a stack of money and asks them to look the other way for an afternoon. I can see it happening."

Shane grunted, staring into the flames.

"What?" Ventura asked.

"Just thinking of how stupid it would be if all of this was just a coincidence. We just stumbled on these Burnt Souls and experiments by accident, and it didn't tie into Bennett."

"Not entirely a coincidence," Ventura said. "Coulson was on this from the beginning."

"Yeah," Shane agreed. "You were just waiting for us in that diner, too, huh?"

Coulson grinned around his cigarette.

"We've been over this, haven't we?" he asked.

"Maybe. Just curious about your real intentions."

"Just what I said. Something is still happening in the PULSE 2 lab."

"But you've never been there, and Doc hasn't been there in years, so how do you know?" Shane asked. "What happened that made you want to come all the way out here?"

"Something took those bodies in Doomtown," Coulson said. "But it wasn't after the bodies. No one needs burned, irradiated skeletons."

"The missing ghosts," Shane said. "But you don't think it was Ross or someone like him."

"No. Nothing like Ross. No one is selling those haunted items," Coulson confirmed.

"Then what?" Shane asked.

Coulson sighed, exhaling a cloud of smoke.

"Something is here," he said, choosing his words carefully even though he had not said anything remarkable. "When I was here before, I heard it. I felt it. But I couldn't see it. It was like... staring into a well. Nothing was there even though something was there."

"Where did you see it? Or not see it, I guess?" Shane asked.

"It's under the ground. It shook the earth like a train. I know it's what dug through the rock and took those ghosts. There's something under the desert out here, and it's not these Burnt Souls or Burners or anything like this. It's not a ghost."

"Well, what does that mean?" Ventura asked. "If it's not a ghost, what is it?"

"That's what I want to find out," Coulson answered.

Ventura shook his head, sitting up and brushing sand off his shirt and pant legs.

"No, it's not as easy as that. What does that mean, not a ghost? What else is there? You're not talking about a goddamn prairie dog."

"I don't know," Coulson said again. "I couldn't see it. I couldn't get a feel from it at all."

Ventura looked at Shane, who shrugged.

"Best not to speculate until we know something," Shane said.

"Why do I feel like you're messing with me?" Ventura asked. "Both of you. Have you ever seen something that wasn't a ghost? Something not human?"

"Ghosts are not always just ghosts," Shane said. "Like these Burnt Souls. I've never heard of anything like this. They're more powerful than almost anything I've encountered, but obviously, not all ghosts work this way. Hell, look at Coulson."

"Yeah, look at me," Coulson agreed.

"Lazarus, the ghost that ran the Iron Tournament, was not just a ghost either," Shane continued. "He was a composite like a ghost cloaked in other spirits. He'd been around for centuries, growing stronger and stronger by absorbing more into himself until he was no longer even a single, thinking entity."

Ventura looked at Coulson.

"Could that be what we're dealing with? Just a… weird ghost? Something no one's seen?"

"I don't know," Coulson repeated. "I have seen things that weren't ghosts, and it doesn't matter to me what it is. What matters is it's dangerous, and it's feeding. It's getting stronger."

"It feeds on the dead?" Ventura asked.

"Looks like it."

"I imagine if it eats the rest of those Burnt Souls that just got released, it's going to get a hell of an energy boost," Shane said.

"Hold on," Ventura said.

He grabbed a rock from the ground and marked an X in the sand.

"Say this is Doomtown," he said. He then drew two more Xs and, after a moment, a handful more. "These are Bunkers 7 and 8, plus the spots where we saw flashes of light from the other Burnt Souls. And this is us here."

He scrawled another X to mark the cave and then looked at his rudimentary map.

"If this maybe-not-a-ghost was in Doomtown, its range is, at most, this circle, right?"

He drew a quick circle in his map with Doomtown as the center and a radius that included several but not all the bunkers.

"Unless it's not a ghost," Coulson countered. "Then a one-mile radius means nothing."

"But if it is, we're well out of range right now. We're out of range of all the bunkers, too. If we keep heading east, we can avoid everything. We're probably already in the Desert National Wildlife Range. Coulson can tell the guards we're hikers before they can get off a shot, and we can get out of here and actually form a plan of attack rather than just stumbling from one near-death experience to another."

"I like this guy; he's a thinker," Coulson turned to Ventura. "But you're missing some details."

"Like what?" Ventura asked.

"That." The ghost pointed past him.

Ventura turned and looked at the mouth of the cave. The sun had long since set, and the night sky was awash with stars. The desert was black and formless beneath them, save for the blinding beam of light that pierced the night southwest of their position like a spotlight.

A second beam of light joined the first, this one wider and not straight. Instead, it arced across the night sky like it was searching for something, sweeping north to south before winking out.

Two more lights joined, sweeping the desert like someone holding the world's brightest flashlight.

"That's out of their range," Ventura said. "There's no way that's within a mile of the bunkers."

He wasn't wrong. Shane was on his feet and quickly kicking dirt over the fire, snuffing the light before anyone could pinpoint them.

"How did they get this close?" Ventura asked.

"It's not the Burnt Souls. Those are the Burners that Eddie told us about. Phase Two," Shane said.

Wherever the Burners were based, it was closer to the rocky hills and their protective cave. And there was every reason to believe they'd already seen the light from their fire.

"We have to get the hell out of here. Now," Shane said.

He turned, facing the cave's interior. It continued into the rocks, though none of them had explored it deeply. Leaving the cave to traverse the rocks in the dark would get them nowhere fast given how close the Burners seemed to be. It was their only option.

Coulson was already heading into the dark. Behind them, a blast of light arced across the sky, and the blinding white beam crossed over the cave, lighting it up until Shane had to shield his eyes and turn away.

He ran after Coulson with Ventura on his heels.

CHAPTER 14
RUN FOR YOUR LIFE

Coulson kept a brisk pace as they descended into the cave. He emitted a soft, blue glow, not as intense as the torchlight he had used in the bunker. This was just enough to prevent either Shane or Ventura from a misstep or a fall.

The cave wound around on a serpentine, unpredictable path until it opened into a wider passageway bolstered by thick, wooden timbers set at regular intervals.

"It's a mine." Coulson stopped and looked left and right down the passage.

The air in the mine was cool but stagnant. Shane heard nothing and, after the winding tunnel through the cave, he was not sure which directions they had to choose from in the mine.

"We need to pick a direction," Ventura said.

Shane could see Coulson deciding which way would take them away from the Burners, but he was having difficulty.

"Left." Shane didn't want to waste any more time on it. Wherever the path took them, it would be away from where they started. That would have to be good enough.

They moved swiftly through the mine, listening to the sounds of their feet on the rocky tunnel floor, scuffing and kicking stones. They reached a junction and had to choose again between a left and right path, opting for the right this time, based on nothing more than a whim.

The air grew colder, and Shane was certain they were going underground. The tunnel sloped almost imperceptibly, but they were definitely going down.

Refuse from the mining operation still lined the tunnels. Old helmets, broken tools, and the odd pair of jeans were scattered about. Coulson even found an ancient pack of Lucky Strikes, the cigarettes inside crumbling to pieces in his hand when he picked them up.

"I don't want to state the obvious, but this is a mine," Ventura said as they descended deeper. "Odds are this comes to a stop somewhere up ahead."

"No, there's air," Coulson said. "Not much, but it's moving. We came in at the back end. We're heading out."

"We're going down, and it's getting deeper," Ventura countered.

Coulson turned to look back at Ventura and smiled. The glow from his skin made him, for the first time since Shane had met him, look like an actual ghost. It was unsettling.

"Trust me," he said, "we're—"

A wail tore through the tunnel, cutting off Coulson. The sound echoed off the walls and was almost vibrating by the time it reached their ears. In another place and time, Shane might have mistaken it for the pained cry of a trapped animal. But there was no doubt here that the Burners had found the cave.

The cry was angry, frustrated, forlorn, and hateful all at once. There was desperation to it, and Shane wondered about the ghost that produced it. Eddie had said the Burners were more precise and controlled. He made them sound more stable than the others, more like Carl or Coulson. If that was the case, the horrible sound chasing them through the dark spoke volumes.

"We've still got a good lead." Coulson felt the tension from the two living men. "They have to find us. These rocks have some iron in them, so they can't just barrel through the walls after us."

"Saved by geology," Ventura said. "Who would have guessed?"

Coulson started forward again, picking up the pace, with Shane and

Ventura right behind. Every so often, another scream reached their ears, and the mineshaft vibrated, knocking streams of dust and small rocks loose.

Even in the cooler air, Shane felt the sweat running down the small of his back. The walls of the mine were close, the shaft had not been built very large, and the ceiling was low.

When the Burners screamed in the distance, dust fell and stuck to the sweat on his head and face, creating a gritty mud that he wiped at with the back of an equally gritty and sweaty hand, smearing it but doing little else. The sounds were drawing closer.

Coulson led them to a new junction, where the path split once again. One tunnel went back to the right; one continued forward. They opted to go straight, but Shane stopped, his eyes focused on the tunnel they were skipping.

"There's something in there," he said, drawing the attention of the other two.

He had seen a fleeting movement, something quick and furtive. It was fast enough that he couldn't say with certainty what it was, only that it was something. But given the place and the encompassing darkness, he didn't need a second look. A ghost was in the tunnel.

"I don't see anything," Coulson said.

"It ran," Shane confirmed. "But it was there."

"Not one of the Burners, right?" Ventura asked.

Shane shook his head.

"Something else. Worry about it when it becomes a problem, I guess," he said.

If they had more time, he would not have been so cavalier. But the fact that it had vanished meant it could be nothing more than a curious spirit that saw them passing and didn't wish to be disturbed. He could think of worse things.

The piercing cry of the Burner echoed down the tunnel again, clearer than ever. The walls shook, and somewhere, the sound of stone collapsing joined the cry, a loud rumble that drowned it out for a moment as the ground shook underfoot.

Coulson said nothing as he started running again. If the Burners didn't catch them, they'd still kill them by bringing the mine down on their heads. They had to find the exit.

Their pace quickened, and the mine changed. The new section was older, and the timbers holding it up were more discolored, weathered, and abundant. Whole sections of walls were covered as though wood paneled.

As they ran, Shane saw gaps in some of the panels that showed not stone but empty space. There were branching passages that had been sealed off. Cold, dead eyes peered out between the spaces in the wood, watching the trio flee the Burners.

Coulson came to a halt just a few yards ahead. The tunnel was floor-to-ceiling wooden slats, some fallen away from the walls and laying dust-covered on the ground. His light extended only a few feet ahead of them, giving everything a soft, blue tinge, and Shane saw nothing move.

He stopped at Coulson's side. No one said anything; they didn't need to. Shane exhaled, and his breath formed a cloud of mist. Behind him, Ventura had already extended an iron baton.

To the right, half the panels had fallen away from a branching tunnel, exposing a black hole in the wall that resisted the glow of Coulson's light. A soft scraping sound came from the darkness like someone dragging something across the dusty ground. It scraped then stopped, scraped then stopped, growing closer to the tunnel each time.

Shane watched a thin, pale hand with swollen knuckles emerge from the shadows, palm down, and claw into the ground as it pulled itself forward. The ghost's body rasped through the dust and grit as the arm pulled the weight behind it until a face emerged into the light, just barely escaping the shadows.

The ghost's head was a fresh burn, red and moist and angry. Its lips had peeled away, shriveled, and rolled up, exposing bloody gums and yellowed teeth. Most of the nose had suffered the same fate, burned to a stub that exposed the sinus cavity inside the spirit's skull.

Milky white eyes leaked fluid down the ghost's raw face in a continuous stream, like tears that dripped from his cheeks and into the dust below. It gasped and clicked its teeth, chattering but not forming words as it pulled free from the tunnel and continued toward them.

Coulson grunted but said nothing. The ghost's other arm had been broken, with the splintered bone cut off just below the shoulder. The ghost had no legs. Its abdomen was a ragged wound trailing intestines and shredded organs behind it.

Every inch of the ghost's exposed body was burned down to the muscle. Its ribs and spine were visible along its back, peeking through the raw mess of seared meat.

It dragged itself toward Coulson, who was closest, and grabbed at him with its hand, clawing at his leg while its teeth chattered. Coulson pushed it away with his boot, forcing it over as though flipping a turtle onto its back, exposing the shredded abdomen that led to its exposed guts. The wounds were not caused by an accident. The tears in the ghost's stomach were intentional. Something had clawed it apart and torn it in half.

Flipped over, Shane saw the ghost's chest and throat had suffered the same fate. It was not speaking, because it lacked the capacity. Its throat had been torn out.

The ghost struggled to right itself using one arm. What had only a moment before been a vision from a nightmare had become something pathetic. Shane watched it push with its good hand, trying to flip over so it could attack again. It would not be a danger to them, as slow and uncoordinated as it was, and he pondered the idea of putting it out of its misery as the humane thing to do.

Before he could decide how to proceed, a second spirit emerged from the tunnel. This one possessed all of its limbs, though it moved on all fours like an animal.

Like the first ghost, this one was badly deformed. It was not covered in the same sorts of burns, but instead looked like it had been malformed from birth. The ghost's mouth was located on the left side of the skull only, as though its jaw had been pulled forward and then broken sharply to one side. The left eye was raised higher than the right as a result, and too much flesh covered its face, such that some of it hung in droopy folds.

The new ghost growled at them. It spoke no words, but the intent was clear. It was angry.

"Behind," Ventura said softly, drawing Shane's attention back the way they had come.

Two more ghosts were in the tunnel, approaching from the rear. One of them was hunched over, not a skeleton but skeletal. It looked like it had died of starvation, with the thin flesh barely covering its body pulled so tight that its joints looked distended and impossibly large. The second spirit was a bloody mess. Something had raked its chest off of its body and exposed the rib cage below.

"We're not looking to cause problems," Ventura said. "Just passing through."

Deep in the mine, the Burner shrieked again. The tunnel shook, and the spirits that approached froze to listen. Shane saw fear in their eyes. It did not look like they had been killed by the Burners—even the burned ghost still had most of its flesh—but they feared them, nonetheless.

"You know what that is." Shane nodded back the way they had come as the anguished sigh died down. "You fear it. Maybe we can fight it together and solve a mutual problem."

The torso ghost chattered its teeth, and the one whose chest had been torn away laughed. The sound was bitter and dry.

No words were spoken, either by inability or a lack of desire. They were not interested in talk. Nor were they interested in helping the trio fight the Burners.

The deformed ghost launched itself at Coulson. Low to the ground as it was, Coulson had to adapt to fight back. He punched it on the top of its head and forced it to the ground, where he stepped on its neck.

"This is a waste of time," he said, pinning the ghost in place.

The deathly thin ghost came for Ventura, but he was swift with the iron baton. Metal hit ghost flesh, and the spirit vanished. Its companion was startled but not dissuaded as it came for Shane.

He punched the ghost in its exposed chest, targeting a spot where the ribs were already fractured. The bone broke and created a hole which Shane quickly grasped at with his other hand, pulling a rib free as he kicked the ghost in the gut and knocked it back.

A burst of cold air caused Shane to turn. Another ghost had emerged from the side tunnel, and there were more behind it. A low moan at his back preceded another spirit coming up the tunnel, and more followed. They moved like a pack of animals, their eyes focused on the living men, and none uttering a word.

Beyond them, lost in darkness, a Burner shrieked again.

CHAPTER 15
THE TUNNEL

One of the wooden support timbers collapsed into the tunnel, bringing a rain of stone with it that fell between Shane and the pursuing spirits, but not enough to block the way. More rubble rained down, and a shard of rock sliced open Ventura's forehead, causing a slow, steady trickle of blood to run down his face.

Coulson bent and picked up the ghost he was standing on, holding it like a sack of potatoes, and rushed toward the previously blocked side tunnel, forcing the ghost back through the hole against its companions.

"Move," he shouted at Ventura and Shane.

Ventura was already running. He swiped at the torso ghost with his iron baton on the way past, clearing their path. Shane was a step behind, heading into the darkness at a full run.

Coulson joined them a moment later, rushing ahead, and lighting the path through the treacherous passageway littered with fallen rocks and timbers. The burned and disfigured ghosts of the mine gave chase, their angry cries and growls following close at their heels.

The deafening cry of a Burner echoed up the passageway again, and a flicker of blinding light strobed through the darkness. It was a single beam, narrow, and reflected off the smooth stone of one of the walls, but it meant the ghost was close.

The ground shook from the sound. Support timbers collapsed, and Shane dodged out of the way, stopping to avoid being crushed as Coulson and Ventura continued ahead of him. A rock larger than a man fell from the ceiling and hit the ground at Shane's feet. The tunnel floor crumbled, and he felt it give way beneath his boots.

The ghosts of the mine had vanished behind him, possibly scared off by the approaching Burner. Shane looked for something to grab as the floor gave out. He clutched at the edge of the rock to find a piece that was still secure, but it flaked away in his hands and fell with him as he tumbled into the darkness.

The dark cavern beneath him was colder than the tunnel above, but it felt different from the mine. The freefall was short, only seconds. He curled up, protecting his head as best he could before he hit the ground, groaning as rock shards embedded themselves in his thighs and back.

Without Coulson around, he was in total darkness. He felt the stone beneath him but nothing else save for the warm sting of blood running from fresh wounds that he ignored as he rode out the pain that shot through his body from the fall.

Seconds passed, and then a light shone on his face. He opened his eyes, staring up at the hole in the ceiling about twenty feet above him. Ventura and Coulson stared down, Coulson glowing more brightly while Ventura held his flashlight.

"Are you all right?" Ventura asked.

"I fell down a hole in a mine," Shane said. "I've been better."

He sat up awkwardly, groaning from dozens of cuts and scrapes, and inspected several. Most had pebbled his back and side and were impossible to see. The ones on his thighs and abdomen were bothersome but not serious. Nothing felt grievously wounded.

"I can come down there." Coulson examined the edge of the hole.

"Why?" Shane said. "You're not flying me out of here. Stay with Ventura. Get out. If there's a way out down here, I'll find it. If not, come back once you've gotten somewhere safe, and the Burners are gone."

"We're not leaving you in a dark cave under a mine full of ghosts," Ventura said.

"No, you're going to give me your flashlight. We've only got a few minutes, and you need to go now."

"They'll find you down there," Ventura warned.

"Just give me the light," Shane said.

Ventura said something under his breath but dropped the light. Shane caught it and flashed it around the new cavern. It was a tunnel like the mine above, but this one had not been made by miners or machines.

"Go," he said. "There's a tunnel. I'll be fine."

The howl of the Burner rang out again from the tunnel above and Coulson pulled Ventura back as more of the rock collapsed. Shane rolled quickly aside to avoid a slab that would have crushed his legs.

The flash of light was brighter and closer this time.

"We're moving," Coulson shouted down. He vanished and Ventura went with him, pulled away by the ghost.

Shane got to his feet, biting back a painful gasp, and started moving. If anything, splitting up could prove helpful. The Burner couldn't pursue them all, and if there was more than one, they'd be split up too. It put the odds back in Shane's favor, and Coulson's as well.

The flashlight beam swept across the new tunnel as Shane hobbled forward to work out a kink in his leg so he could walk or even run properly again. He turned back after a moment, shining the light up to the hole in the ceiling. The lipless face of the chattering torso ghost stared at him with its milky eyes, hanging upside down like a bat. It did not pursue him into the new tunnel, but it watched.

If the ghost was not giving chase, it didn't matter. Shane ignored it and turned back to the way he was headed. The tunnel seemed to follow the same direction as the mine ahead. It appeared as though it had been dug more recently. There was something new about the way the rock looked and even felt. Edges seemed almost freshly hewn and were still sharp.

The cuts in the stone were irregular, not like they had been made with a drilling machine or even pickaxes. They looked rougher. From floor to ceiling, the rounded tunnel bore the same markings in the rock like gouges, as if someone had chiseled it. It was far too large for that though, easily twice the size of the mineshaft above.

Shane stopped after a few dozen yards to pull a rock fragment from the back of his leg. It was embedded just below his knee and had made running more difficult. The pain was worse when he removed it, but his leg worked better.

He leaned on a wall, flexing his leg, and ensuring the bleeding was not too bad. With the flashlight held between his teeth, he tore free a section of his shirt and used it to bind the wound, keeping pressure on to staunch the bleeding.

The wall under his fingers was cold and lined with smooth grooves. He shifted his weight and his hand slid almost perfectly into place.

Now that *seemed familiar*, he thought, turning his head to inspect the rock face more closely.

His hand had settled into a handprint that had been gouged into the wall. The finger width was almost a perfect match for his. The length was slightly off, but that could have been because the hand that had made the print had scraped through the rock like it was putty rather than solid stone.

Shane took the light in his other hand and moved it slowly along the curved wall. From the floor to the ceiling, he saw places where whole hands or just a few fingers had torn the rock apart. In some places, the edges were smooth and rounded like heat had been applied, or like the hand had been molten hot when it grasped the stone and pulled it apart.

His first thought was that one of the Burners must have carved the tunnel, but that didn't make sense. If they could burn hot enough to melt stone, why would they not just melt all the way through? Why would they use their hands? And as he inspected the marks more closely, marks that rose to a ceiling several feet above his head, it was clear that several hands had made them. This was not the work of one being, ghost, or man. Dozens of hands had worked together.

Shane stood still, staring at the ceiling above him and the clear handprint in the rock. The ceiling must have been ten feet above him. Why would anyone have climbed up on something and boosted themselves up just to gouge their way through stone to make a tunnel? What reason would they have to make it so big?

Behind him, where he had fallen into the tunnel, Shane heard a rock tumble to the ground. It was only one, clattering to the tunnel floor from the hole above. He turned the flashlight toward the sound but could no longer see the pile of rubble where he had fallen.

No other noise accompanied the falling stone. There was no scream from the Burner and no angry growls from the ghosts that made the mine their home. Nothing moved in the beam of his light. There was only the stone of the tunnel and the handmade thing he found himself in, which mirrored the mine above for unknown reasons.

He would get no answers by waiting for something to come for him. Shane turned away from the wall and followed the tunnel, making his leg work despite the pain. He forced himself to stretch and bend the muscles as he sped up until he reached a slow jog.

The pain was sharp, and he winced, teeth clenched and sweat beading across his forehead and down his back. The alternative was to wait for the Burner, and he could not allow that to happen. He would make his leg work whether the wounds liked it or not.

The scream of one of the Burners echoed off the stone walls. The sound was deafening, forcing Shane to cover his ears as he turned and looked back the way he had come. The blinding white light fell in a shaft from the hole through which she had fallen, illuminating the tunnel below it like an overhead spotlight in a theater.

Shane expected the ghost to follow, to drop down like a falling star, blazing white light and raging fire in pursuit of him. The light faded instead, slowly at first, and then as though a switch had gone off.

The after-image of the light glowed purple in his vision, and he continued to flee but the ghost did not appear. Like the angry spirits of the mine, it would not enter the tunnel to come after him.

The seconds ticked by, and Shane continued to run through the tunnel, barely paying attention to the ground illuminated by the flashlight as he continued to look over his shoulder. Each step saw him running alone and fleeing from nothing. The Burner was not coming after him.

Shane was relieved that he was not being pursued. With the state he was in and the layout of the tunnel, he would not be able to easily get the drop on one of the Burners before it used its abilities against him. On the other hand, he wondered why none of the ghosts wanted to enter the tunnel.

It seemed clear now that a Burner had not forged the tunnel. Something else had made it, and none of the spirits wanted anything to do with it. Shane was reminded of their visit to Doomtown. Something below the earth had pulled the remains of the dead down, digging through the earth to do so. Coulson believed that something in the ground was feeding on the dead. If the other ghosts were afraid to enter the tunnel, maybe they believed the same.

Shane forged onward. The tunnel had to go somewhere. It had breached the surface in the mine, so he was certain that it had to do so somewhere else.

But if he could not find a way out before he found what made the tunnel, he might very well never see daylight again.

Chapter 16
What Lies Beneath

The tunnel maintained a consistent diameter for most of Shane's journey. Ten feet or so around indicated whatever had created the hole was massive compared to a living man. The idea that whatever had made it was waiting in the dark somewhere was at the forefront of Shane's mind, but he pressed on.

The Burners had not followed him, but he didn't think they had given up on their hunt. Coulson and Ventura were the targets now, and Shane didn't know how much Coulson could protect Ventura from what was coming.

No more sounds came from above, no pained shrieks or ominous rumblings. Shane thought that in a way, that was even worse. It left him fumbling through darkness with no idea if he was on the right track or if his friends were still in danger.

The light from his flashlight bobbed as he ran, flashing back and forth across forgettable, ridged stone until suddenly, the walls of the tunnel came to an end in an open cavern.

Whatever had clawed the tunnel out of the rock had found a natural cave below the ground and broken through. A small amount of rubble lay at the entrance, but any sign of whatever had dug the passage ended there.

For the first time, as Shane turned to look back, he realized there had been no rubble in the tunnel. A few small, stray stones and pebbles, but nothing else. What had it done with all the rock it moved?

Shane turned back to the cavern and swept the space with his light. The ceiling was much higher here, meaning either the passage above had gone up or he had gone deeper into the earth. He was at least twenty feet from the natural roof of the cavern and the jagged stalactites that hung from it.

The cavern spread wide and away from the burrowed tunnel and glistened with a faint moisture when he swept the light across the exposed stones. It was strange to think of damp caves beneath the desert. He wondered how far underground he was.

He made out a path across the cavern, a groove dug into the stone that had knocked some stalagmites and rocky formations out of the way.

The passage of whatever had burrowed the tunnel through the rock had continued, unfazed by the cavern, on a straight path to the far side. Shane's exit was waiting for him, but the cavern was not empty.

To the side of the burrowed path was a body. The remains were old, but the cold of the cavern had preserved some of the flesh and it had not yet been reduced to bone. The flesh was like jerky, but the body was not like anything Shane had ever seen.

At first, he thought it was two corpses together, but as he got closer, running the beam of the flashlight across it as he crouched next to it, he realized that was not the case. Or at least, not exactly. There were parts from two bodies, but they had merged.

For a moment, Shane considered the possibility that he was looking at conjoined twins, but the way the bodies were merged would not allow for it. In some places where they were exposed, the bones looked like they had melted together, fused like they were made of wax and pushed into one another under heat.

The leathery flesh was like webbing across some parts of the body, connecting legs and arms in ways they should never have been. The two skulls were almost entwined, one facing forward and one facing back. They were bonded with a clear seam from front to back, and patches of dried skin grew from one to the other.

Whatever Shane was looking at, it had been forced together at the most basic level. The bones were not just stuck, they were growing out of each other. The flesh looked to be covering both bodies as one. It looked like the fats, collagen, and very minerals that made up the tissue and bone had been amalgamated into one thing across the two bodies until they became one.

Shane couldn't imagine it had ever been alive in the state that he saw it, nor could he imagine any power that could have forced two living beings together in such a way.

Shane was still inspecting the combined heads of the corpses when he heard a faint shuffling in the darkness. He swung the light toward the sound and watched as a spirit hobbled between some shattered stalagmites toward him.

The ghost was that of the wretched thing Shane was crouched next to. His inability to imagine it as a living thing was quickly remedied as he watched it moving impossibly in ghostly form. Flesh and bone were exposed in equal parts, and the fused portions of its conjoined body made it unthinkable yet real all at once.

The joints were not just bonded but broken, working at angles that would never have worked for a living thing. The heads were bound facing opposite ways, but one torso had been twisted around so that the arms bent backward in a broken embrace around the body of the first, and the legs pushed through to the far side through its open abdomen.

It walked, as much as it could be called walking, on three arms and two legs. The other limbs were not positioned to reach the ground, especially the two legs that stuck out of what was essentially the thing's back.

One face looked at Shane, but only with a single eye, as the other was trapped within the skull of the second head that faced up. The bone and flesh on the ghost looked alive, unlike the decayed version on the ground next to him. This flesh was pink and red, scourged with burns but still pulsing with life and blood and yellowed blister serum.

The pain in the ghost's eye was unmistakable. Shane had rarely seen such anguish. Whatever had killed the spirit and forced it into the inexplicable bonding with a second, had trapped it in its most painful moment of life. It now existed like that eternally.

"What did this to you?" Shane asked softly.

The single eye, blood-red and strangely swollen, stared at him as the broken jaw, free from the neighboring skull, worked and rotated as though remembering how to speak. Instead, it only produced a series of rattles and choking sounds.

The second face moaned atop the thing's body, producing a series of cries like a wounded animal, long vowels that sounded forlorn and pathetic.

Thick drool tainted with blood sputtered out over the spirit's swollen lips. It lurched toward Shane, its movements unsteady and awkward as it maintained balance. It was not fast or elegant, but it had picked up speed and was coming for him.

Shane got to his feet, setting the flashlight to one side. He didn't know how to approach the thing or how to defend against an attack from two bodies twisted as one. There was no tactic for this, and no experience to prepare him.

"We don't have to do this," he said.

The second head wailed again, a keening sound like a hurt dog. This head had both eyes, but they were burned and blind, white and black like something hot had been gouged into them.

Shane kept the thing at a distance, hoping he could reason with it or at least convince it that fighting was not a good strategy. It did not give him any sign to suggest that it could still reason or even understand his words.

The free hand on the spirit's side grabbed at Shane, digging nails into his leg as both heads tried to bite him. With one arm holding him steady, the ghost pulled itself almost upright, climbing Shane's body the way a dog might get to its hind legs.

The underside of the ghost had yet another arm. Shane counted five now and nothing about the ghost made sense to him. It was desperate and angry, and that was all that mattered.

The bottom head rasped, spitting blood in his face and trying to bite his cheek. Shane caught it before it was close enough with a hand on the ghost's throat to keep it at bay.

Because of how it had joined the second body, Shane could not get his hand around the ghost's neck, he could only hold it back. Two more arms clawed at him now, and both heads chattered and moaned, sounds that were instinct and emotion with no thought behind them.

Shane knocked one of the monster's legs out from under it, toppling the whole thing. It lost its grip in two hands but maintained the third at Shane's collar. He didn't resist and instead fell with it, using its greater bulk to get more leverage as he grasped the one-eyed head between his hands and crushed it as they hit the ground.

The second head shrieked as the skull collapsed, crunching into a pulpy mass in Shane's hands. A burst of energy buffeted Shane like a full-body tackle, and he coughed, falling back against a stalagmite as he caught his breath.

Shane was briefly stunned as hands took hold of him once more, blindly now but still energetically. The spirit had not been destroyed. He had only wounded it.

Cold, jagged fingernails raked through his shirt and down his chest, and Shane winced. His hesitation had cost him, and the spirit was still fighting.

Shane repositioned himself, driving a knee into the ghost's warped torso and causing it to bend sharply. The second head lurched back, and though he could not see its face, it didn't matter. He clutched the skull, one hand grasping where the first skull had shattered and the other on the smooth outside, and pushed again, forcing the bone to give way.

One final, pathetic wail escaped the spirit's lips before the skull crumbled in on itself and then pulsed with a surge of explosive energy. Shane was knocked back again, but he saw in the beam of the flashlight that the ghost had not been destroyed. Most of the limbs fumbled now, but the fifth arm was dragging the body toward Shane while the legs on the back still kicked.

"What the hell are you?" Shane muttered, wiping blood from his mouth as he regained his footing.

The ghost stumbled and rolled, flipping over as it came toward him. Shane saw exposed ribs from the backside. Trapped within them, a pair of yellow and red eyes stared out. A third head had been fused into the mix, another body swallowed by the first two, buried in the torso of the monster and just barely exposed.

Shane swore out loud, watching as the ghost moved toward him. Without the two other heads, it had lost a great deal of function, but it retained enough to keep moving.

He stopped it as it lurched toward him and took the functional arm, breaking it swiftly and then rolling the body, so the exposed ribs faced him. Shane then drove an elbow into the ribs with a frustrated growl, breaking several. He pried the bones out of his way to expose the head hidden inside, stripped almost entirely of flesh. It gnashed its teeth as Shane's hands came close, unable to defend itself any other way. The eyes stared into Shane's and all he saw was madness. Whatever humanity the thing once had was long gone.

Shane said nothing as he clutched the raving, hidden skull and pressed down hard. The bone shattered more easily than the others, as though the merging process had weakened it the most, and the ghost split apart in a spray of bone and tissue that vanished nearly instantly.

When Shane hit the ground this time, he was quick to regain his footing, even with the wind knocked out of him. He gasped for air in the darkness and reached for the flashlight, sweeping across the cavern. The ghost was gone now. The body was shattered as well, broken to bits and ragged scraps of leathery flesh.

Shane did not understand what the spirit was or what could have made it. But it had many hands, and it was bulkier than a man. He turned the beam of the light toward the tunnel, the one dug by multiple hands. The thing he destroyed could not have made the tunnel, but perhaps something like it had. Something made of more bodies. Many more bodies, and much bigger. Maybe something like that could have done it.

If such a thing existed.

Chapter 17
Fire Down Below

═══

Coulson was a half-dozen paces ahead, running through the tunnel like it was his morning jog and he had the route memorized. Ventura struggled to keep up, breathing heavily but saying nothing. The ghost had no oxygen in his lungs, no lactic acid burning in his muscles, and no reason to slow down or feel exhausted. He could probably run forever.

Ventura would not yell for the ghost to slow down or wait for him. He didn't want to give Coulson the satisfaction, for one. But more than that, he was relieved to have the pace set by something that had no reason to slow. It motivated him to push harder. If he slowed or stumbled, he would die.

They had lost Ryan he had no idea how far back. The tunnel took a circuitous route that weaved like a snake. It could have been a mile or more of running for only a few hundred yards of forward progress.

The ghosts from the mine had followed them, appearing at random intervals from adjacent tunnels. Coulson passed the tunnels without slowing, saying they were not worth exploring, and a ghost would appear a moment later. Ventura used the iron baton clutched in his fist against those bold enough to attack. Coulson simply punched them.

The fear that the Burner at their heels might have dropped down after Ryan into the mysterious cavern below the mineshaft quickly abated when the howl from the dead thing shook the walls, loosening more stone and timber.

Because of the weaving tunnels, the light no longer reached them. Even reflecting off the walls, it only traveled so far, and they looped through the mine far too frequently for any direct light to reach them. It was a blessing in that Ventura didn't need to worry about a searing shaft of nuclear fire igniting his head from behind. It also made him more nervous, as the ghost could have been only a few paces away.

The mine's cool air made it easier to run than out in the open desert, but that didn't count for much. What they needed more than anything was distance. He had no idea how far they needed to go to escape the grasp of the Burners, but they were not there yet.

Soon, it became clear that the mine tunnel was angling up, and running became more of a struggle. The incline was far from steep, but it put more pressure on Ventura's exhausted legs. A day of walking in the desert with minimal water had left him in less than peak condition.

He knew Ryan had been a Marine. He was trained and conditioned to handle rough conditions. He was a survivor. Plus, he had dealt with ghosts for a lot longer than Ventura had. Or at least it seemed that way. The man had not spoken much of his past, but the way he handled himself led Ventura to believe Ryan had more than a few years of fighting the dead under his belt.

This was all new to Ventura. Even though he'd seen ghosts since he was a child, he had spent most of his life avoiding them. Seeing them without seeing them, and not letting them know that he knew. He had avoided the issue and now maybe that was to his detriment. Maybe if he'd learned more, or accepted it instead of denying it, he would be better prepared.

He knew he was being stupid. Shane Ryan could physically fight ghosts; Ventura could not. Nothing could have prepared him for what he was doing except a stronger focus on cardio workouts. He'd make up for it if he survived.

Coulson had come to a stop ahead of him. Ventura was thankful for the break but also wary as he caught up to the ghost where the tunnel opened into a small clearing set up with an ancient-looking shack and the end of a track for mine cars that continued down another tunnel.

"This was a refuge chamber," Coulson said. "Or an early version of one."

He pointed to the shack and a pipe that extended into the rock above. It must have been drilled to the surface to provide for fresh air. Presumably, before anyone was dropping nuclear weapons in the desert.

"Does that mean we're close to getting out of here?" he asked.

"Closer than we were," Coulson said. "But I don't think they built these right next to any exits. We might be getting close to the mine shaft, the cage, the elevator, and that whole thing."

"Elevator?" Ventura said. He hadn't considered that they'd need to go straight up to get out. There was no way an elevator would still work after all this time.

"Relax; there's got to be a ladder. Be more worried that the cage collapsed with timber and mine cars in it, and there's no way out of here except the way we came in."

"Yeah," Ventura said, still breathing heavily. "I'll worry about that now."

He wanted to get going again. As badly as his legs and lungs burned, he didn't want his flesh to burn, too. They could rest outside, with a mile between them and the cave they had entered. Then they could plan on how to go back and find Ryan.

Coulson was not moving, so Ventura took the initiative to head out. He saw the tunnel lead onward, lined with tracks for the mine cars. He wondered if it would help them if the tracks were iron and would keep the ghosts at bay.

The ghost took a step alongside Ventura and put out a hand, stopping the living man from proceeding.

"Not yet," Coulson said softly.

He nodded into the darkness and extended his free hand. The light he produced intensified and spread, pushing back the shadows and revealing a pair of ghosts huddled next to the tracks, watching them.

The spirits were pressed to the stone walls as if trying to blend in with them. One was swollen all over, its flesh pink and glistening like it had suffered a full-body allergic reaction. The other was desiccated, like it had died under the desert sun, with a massive, dark-stained hole in its chest that exposed black innards.

A third ghost lumbered out of the shack, this one almost passing as alive, save for the deathly pale flesh and sunken eyes.

Ventura readied his baton. He was not sure why the ghosts in the mine were so hell-bent on attacking them, but they were unwilling to communicate, and time was limited. He wished he'd brought some more weapons with him. He had gloves studded with iron that he was sure would be more effective than iron knuckles. A few more bags of iron shavings wouldn't have hurt, either. He had two in his pockets, but the baton was at least effective against the spirits that couldn't melt it.

As if on cue, the harsh screech of the Burner pursuing them echoed through the mine tunnel, causing the floor and ceiling to shake. The ghosts in the refuge reacted angrily, the pale one that was closest full-on attacking as soon as it heard the sound.

Coulson caught the spirit in both hands, lifted it with its own momentum, and slammed it back against the wall of the wooden shack, breaking a hole through it and causing the structure to collapse.

"Move," Coulson yelled.

Ventura did not need to be told twice. He ran toward the track-lined tunnel even as the swollen, red ghost and his dried-out partner came at him. He hit the swollen ghost first as it was the larger target, taking a swipe at the puffy, pink flesh of its face. It either didn't realize what Ventura held or didn't care as it made no effort to defend itself. The iron hit the ghost's head and banished it.

The tunnel behind him shook violently, and the wooden shack exploded outward as Coulson stood. He had destroyed the ghost and was now following Ventura, moving at a blinding speed.

Coulson reached the ghost before Ventura did, plunging his hand into the other ghost's head and lifting it by its face. He smashed the ghost on the rock wall of the tunnel, and it shattered like glass, exploding with a force that pushed Coulson back but did not knock him over.

Ventura rushed past him, and the two ran up the tunnel that ascended more steeply than the previous one. The tracks provided more footing, and he used them to brace himself as he ran.

Guttural moans and growls pursued them. Ventura did not look back to see what gave chase; it was enough to know the ghosts of the mine were after them.

They rounded a bend, and Ventura felt his chest tighten. The smell of the desert hit his nose for the first time since they'd entered the mine. It was earthy but also slightly floral. He'd never considered how a desert smelled, but it was unmistakable now that he smelled it again.

"There." Coulson pointed ahead.

It was as he had predicted. A cage and an ancient steam-powered elevator from at least a hundred years ago. But the shaft went up, and the desert wind brought the fresh air down to them. All they had to do was climb to reach it.

Ventura couldn't gauge the height of the shaft as he approached. It vanished into the stone ceiling, but in the soft, blue glow of Coulson's light, he saw a wooden ladder fixed to the wall alongside the shaft. It looked as ancient as everything else, but it had been built solid. He hoped the wood had weathered the years well.

Coulson dropped back and took on another ghost that had caught up with them, something Ventura hadn't even seen. He dispatched it quickly, this time falling to the ground when it came apart and the blast of spiritual energy washed over him.

"Coulson," Ventura said, stopping when he saw his companion take a fall. More ghosts came up the tunnel behind them, the first bounding forward like a dog and leaping on Coulson while he was still down.

"Climb! I'll be there when I'm done."

He caught the ghost before it could bite his throat and landed a powerful blow into its mouth, shattering the teeth it had tried to use as weapons.

A second ghost reached him, this one a man still dressed in his helmet and coveralls, a miner who had been crushed somewhere judging from his broken body.

Ventura wanted to go back and help Coulson, but more were coming up the tunnel. As he struggled with his desire to fight, a blast of white light seared his vision, lighting up the tunnel like it was midday.

The Burner shrieked again, and the tunnel shook. The cage groaned and rattled, and rocks fell from above.

"What the hell are you doing?" Coulson yelled.

Ventura swore and turned his back on his companion, running for the wooden ladder. He grabbed hold and looked up, seeing only blackness waiting for him, and then, from the tiny hole far above his head, a night sky dotted with stars.

He must have been several hundred feet down, but there was nowhere else to go, and no faster way to escape. Ventura started climbing.

The sound of another ghost coming apart followed him, shaking the mine, and rattling loose more stones. Moments later, another rumbled the wall on which the ladder was fixed, and then another.

Ventura climbed as fast as he could. The wooden planks of the ladder were dry and brittle. Sometimes, a nail squealed as it loosened under his weight, and all he could do was reach for the next one and hope it held stronger. They shifted and wobbled when the mine shaft was rocked by another burst of energy. Coulson, unseen somewhere below, was still tearing apart the dead.

Five explosions shook the mine shaft, then a sixth, and a seventh. Each one rained debris on Ventura's head. He climbed as fast as his arms and legs allowed.

He was more than halfway up the shaft when the howl of the Burner sounded again. Ventura's guts tightened, and he forced himself to look down. It was so close now that he thought it was climbing after him. Instead, he watched as the darkness below brightened and the light filled the mine shaft so intensely that he had to look away and climb up.

Hot air chased him like a blast from an oven being opened swiftly. It stung the exposed flesh on his arms and face. The Burner was in the room with Coulson, it had just set off a blast of energy, and he had no idea if his companion had the power to withstand it.

A plank from the ladder pulled free in his hands and Ventura nearly fell, catching himself on the next plank just in time as the other tumbled to the bottom of the shaft. He swore and looked down. The light from below had faded, and there was nothing to see. He heard the plank hit the ground with a rattle and a thump, and then everything was silent.

Anger pushed him forward as much as fear. He had not wanted to abandon Ryan or Coulson. If the ghost had died or been destroyed, or whatever happened to spirits, just to protect Ventura's escape…

The idea of it enraged him. His job was to protect others. He was the one who put his life on the line, not the people with him. It was not acceptable that Ryan and Coulson might have both been lost, and he was the one escaping. The one who had no power to stop what they were there to stop in the first place. He had no right to be the one who got away.

Ventura continued his climb, ignoring the pain that screamed through his body and the exhaustion that threatened to steal the strength from his hands. He shouldn't have been the one to live.

But if he was, he would make sure someone paid for what happened to his companions.

CHAPTER 18

MISLAID PLANS

Cold sand shifted under Ventura's hand. He pulled himself up from the mine shaft, pushing off the final wooden step, and then flopped onto his back, staring up at the night sky.

It was cool, and the gentle breeze felt like a godsend against the sweat that covered his body. He breathed deeply, and all his muscles relaxed. He felt like he would never be able to move again.

He could have fallen asleep right there and let the coyotes take him at that moment. He was just glad to be free of the mine and the pursuing spirits.

But he wasn't free. Or he might not have been. He had no idea. He could have been out of range of the Burners, or he could have had another half-mile of running ahead of him. He was not sure how far he had traveled or where the Burners were based. For all he knew, he had traveled in a circle underground and ended up back where he started.

He couldn't rest. Shane Ryan was still somewhere underground. Coulson might still be down there, too. And someone was still operating a secret facility in the desert that allowed radioactive remains out into the world. He had work to do.

Something cold and firm grasped Ventura by the ankle and pulled. He screamed, as much from surprise as fear, and clawed at the stony, sandy ground as it dragged him back toward the mine shaft.

He reached into his pocket, struggling for the iron baton he'd slipped in there during his climb. The cold metal butted against his fingertips and he grasped it quickly, pulling it free as he lifted his head to face his attacker and get some leverage to free himself.

Coulson grinned at him around a cigarette and released his ankle.

"What are you doing, sleeping up here?" he said as he climbed out of the mine.

"Jesus Christ." Ventura gasped, his heart thumping in his chest.

The ghost stood at the edge of the shaft and looked down the way he had come.

"Not exactly, but I guess I am a dead guy coming out of a cave," he replied.

"Stop with the jokes. What happened? I thought that Burner caught up with you and… I don't know."

"You thought I died," Coulson said.

"You're already dead," Ventura said, a fact Coulson had just brought up.

"Good thing, too, or that guy would have killed me. Had to duck behind a mine car for a second until he turned the light show off."

"You destroyed it?" Ventura asked.

Coulson nodded, taking the cigarette from between his lips and looking around. They were in a small canyon with a sheer rock wall to their right and a path to their left.

Scrub and gnarled trees grew around them, and aside from the ancient wooden frame built over the mine shaft and another half-collapsed shack, there was nothing there.

"Are you okay?" Ventura asked.

It was unclear just how much damage Coulson could take. Maybe he didn't even know.

"Coulson?"

The ghost was staring at some twisted pinyon pines growing among the rocks. The cigarette in his hand burned bright despite neither being real nor in his mouth.

"On your feet, Agent," he said softly, not bothering to look at the living man.

Ventura stared into the darkness. To his eyes, the trees were just dark outlines on a dark background. Light from the night sky and an abundance of stars were more illuminating than the tunnels below, but they didn't offer much.

Ventura got up, still clutching the iron baton, and watched as a soft, white light grew brighter behind the closest tree. Coulson tossed his cigarette, and a second light joined the first. Then a third, and a fourth.

The four Burners formed a line, walking out from beyond the trees and increasing their brightness to the point that it was nearly impossible to see the faces of the ghosts beneath it. But they stopped before the light became blinding, restraining their abilities.

Between them, a fifth ghost approached, cast in the light of its companions. The ghost was a man, bent badly under a hunched back that swelled and bulged obscenely around a segment of exposed spine.

The man's face was a roadmap of lines, wrinkles upon wrinkles like he had spent his life frowning at the sun and suffered the consequences. His hair hung from one side of his head only; the side with the hunch was bald and oddly smooth compared to his heavily wrinkled visage.

Despite the state of his back, he wore clothing. Most of a suit jacket covered him, except for where his back bulged through in a section that had melted and merged with his flesh, making the garment a permanent addition to his body.

His gait was painful to watch, but he kept his eyes locked on Coulson and Ventura, no sign that he was struggling or bothered. Deformed as he was, Ventura thought at first that he might be one of the spirits from the mine, but he quickly changed his mind. Something was different about this ghost.

The Burners seemed to be deferring to the hunched-over ghost, holding back on their abilities and serving as bodyguards. They stopped walking when he stopped walking, and Ventura scanned their faces. Their features were obscured in the diffuse white light. He could make out the shadows of eyes, lips on some, and a skeletal jaw on another. But nothing defined.

"Where is the third man?" the hunched ghost asked. His voice had a hint of a Russian accent but was otherwise unremarkable. He spoke the words as though asking for directions.

"Who's asking?" Coulson said.

The hunched ghost squinted at him, cocking his head.

"You are bold; I give you that. Stupid, maybe?"

"Mom always said I had lots of potential," Coulson replied. The hunched ghost ignored the comment and focused on Ventura.

"Where is the third man?"

"Dead," Ventura answered. "Fell into a cavern and broke his neck."

"A cavern?" the hunched spirit said.

Ventura saw the gears working as the ghost considered his words. That meant something to him, but it was unclear if it was good or bad.

"And you two survived. You two survived the spirits of the mine. You two escaped a Burnt Soul and triggered the Burners. You two just run across this desert like it's your backyard, hmm?"

"Thinking of moving here. Dry climate, lots of space," Coulson said. "Neighbors are assholes, but what are you going to do?"

"How?" the ghost said. "How do you do these things?"

"What things?" Coulson asked.

"How do you survive what cannot be survived? That you can even see me is remarkable, yes? Did you know that fewer than two percent of the population can see spirits? And of those, only the smallest fraction realizes what it sees? You two are not here by mistake. You came here for the dead. You sell them like the others? Barter in death for cash the American way?"

The ghost chuckled and shook his head as if the question had been asked to him instead of by him.

"No, you are not traffickers. You come here for something else."

Coulson folded his arms across his chest and shrugged.

"Hell, sounds like you've got all the answers, you don't even need us."

"No. No, I do not need you," the ghost agreed. "I do not believe your friend is dead. I do not believe you are here by accident. And I do not believe you should survive any longer."

"You wouldn't be the first ghost who thought he could kill me." Ventura's fist tightened around the iron baton. "Doubt you'll be the last."

"So bold," the hunchback said. "Did they send you here because you were a brave man? Or because you were a stupid man?"

"Come find out," the agent said.

Coulson laughed, grinning at Ventura before reaching into his coat to pull out a cigarette for the first time since they'd met. It occurred to him then that the hunchback had not realized Coulson was not alive. His disguise was so good that even other ghosts fell for it.

"*Ubit ikh*," the ghost said in Russian.

The Burners surrounding them moved in. Their light was bright but had not yet taken on the intense glow. There was no heat, either. It was just as Eddie had told them, these ones had more control and precision in how they handled their ability. That also meant they were vulnerable.

Ventura plunged his hands into his pockets, gouging his fingers into the bags he had stuffed in them before they had left Benton. The plastic tore, and tiny, jagged pieces of metal spilled into his waiting palms. He closed his fingers around the sharp little pieces and pulled out two handfuls.

He said nothing as he swung his arms wide. Had the Burners increased their heat, they would have melted the tiny shavings long before they made contact, but the ghosts had not. A cascade of metal arced through the air and speckled the four glowing spirits. The lights vanished in the blink of an eye and all four were gone, leaving the hunchback alone.

The spirit cursed in Russian, his gaze darting furtively from Coulson to Ventura and back.

"Iron, yes? A parlor trick. It only delays the inevitable. You are miles from safety. You will die screaming in these sands, and only I will hear you begging for mercy," the ghost said.

"You're a cocky little fella, I'll give you that," Coulson said. "But I don't know if I'd be so confident without your backup dancers."

"I don't need them to gut you and watch your blood soak into the earth."

The hunchback stalked toward Coulson, his wrinkled face twisting in a rage-filled snarl as he reached a small, deformed hand for Coulson's stomach as though he meant to make good on his threat then and there.

Coulson waited for the ghost as calmly as could be and then took him by the wrist when he was close enough, catching the hand before it made contact and holding it firmly.

The hunchback ghost's eyes widened and the look of shock on his face was enough to make Ventura laugh despite the seriousness of the situation. He had not expected any manner of defense. He had not predicted Coulson.

"How about you tell us what's in the PULSE lab?" Coulson leaned down so he was face-to-face with the ghost. "Who's running it, what they're doing, and where it is."

The hunchback laughed in Coulson's face.

"You want the laboratory? You came all this way for the PULSE experiment? You should let me kill you now. I do you a favor!"

He laughed louder and Coulson frowned, punching the ghost in the face as he let his wrist go.

The hunchback fell to the ground. Coulson lifted his foot to stomp on the other spirit's head but the ghost moved with a surprising quickness, scuttling not away but forward, lunging at Coulson and knocking his legs out from under him.

Coulson fell back and the hunchback clambered up his body, lifting his crooked little hand to swipe at his face.

"You'll never leave this place alive," the ghost growled.

"He's not alive, idiot," Ventura said, cracking the end of the iron baton down on the top of the ghost's head.

The hunchback vanished, and Coulson was left on his back, staring up at Ventura's face. The ghost laughed and made no move to get on his feet.

"He's not alive, idiot," Coulson said in a fair approximation of Ventura's voice. "Oh my God, that was so good. That was like something Schwarzenegger would have said in the early nineties before, well, bashing in a guy's head with an iron bar. Well done."

He got to his feet and clapped Ventura on the shoulder. The cigarette was back in his mouth.

"That was something," he said.

"We should go before they get back," Ventura said.

He took out the Burners by surprise. It would not work a second time, especially with only the loose bits of iron he had in his pockets.

"Yeah," Coulson agreed. "Although you have to wonder how they knew we'd be coming out here. And who Quasimodo is to be ordering Burners around. Maybe looking for him isn't such a bad idea."

"I don't think we come out on top if we go a second round," Ventura said.

"No," Coulson said. "Good job with the iron filings, by the way. Very dramatic. You have a real action-movie vibe that you didn't have earlier today. It's working for you."

"Coulson," Ventura said. He'd spend a few hours driving back to Vegas sharing jokes with the ghost when they were done if he wanted to. Now, he just wanted to stay alive.

"I gotcha," the ghost said. He turned in a circle, looking across the night sky, and then chose a seemingly random path to their left, away from the canyon.

"More cover that way. We'll stay out of sight and wait to see if our friend comes back. If he does, we follow. If he doesn't, we work on a way to find Ryan."

"You think he's still alive?" Ventura asked as they started their hike away from the mine shaft.

"Shane Ryan? Hell, I couldn't kill him. Doubt anything under this desert will."

CHAPTER 19
LIGHT AND DARK

The tunnel had become erratic. Whatever had dug it out of the rock had weaved back and forth as though zigzagging aimlessly. Shane couldn't guess what it was doing or what had motivated it. The effort and the power to do such a thing seemed so great that wasting the time to dart back and forth instead of taking a straightforward path made no sense.

The only thing Shane surmised was that the tunneler had actively pursued something and that thing, whatever it was, eluded capture by taking a random path.

It was not the most satisfying explanation, but it was the best he could come up with. In the end, it didn't matter why something had dug the tunnel, he just hoped it had dug it to a conclusion that saw it break the surface. It had to come out somewhere, even if it was just another collapsed tunnel that connected to it. Anything Shane could use to escape and return to the surface.

Shane had seen no other bodies or other spirits since the thing he discovered in the cavern. The ghost he had destroyed weighed on his mind, though. The idea that something could have been made from combining multiple ghosts did not mesh with how ghosts were created or existed based on his experience.

He had met ghosts that had suffered horrible fates, and they had returned as impossible beings, disfigured beyond words and barely human, but their bodies did not match the trauma that their spirits gave form to. Nor did they include others. A ghost was the spirit of a once-living thing, a specific and individual entity. It was a pure form, a person's essence, corrupted though it might have been in death. It was all that remained of one living being. How it could join with others just... defied reason.

Shane could not keep the idea from his mind that the tunneler, the thing in whose footsteps he walked, was a more complex, horrifying, version of what he had destroyed. But to be large enough to do that, it would have to have been made of dozens of bodies. It would have to have been a horror unlike anything he had imagined. The most impossible thing. He would not believe it without seeing it for himself. And in his heart, Shane had no desire to see such a thing.

Since destroying the fused ghost, Shane had only heard his footfalls in the tunnel, boots on stone that created a faint echo with each step. The cries of the Burner in the tunnel above had ended some time ago. He liked to think Coulson had destroyed it, but he knew it was just as likely that the ghost had reached the limit of its ability to pursue. There was also the chance it had destroyed Coulson, but Shane would not entertain that as a serious possibility. Depowered though the ghost might have been, Shane didn't see him dying in a nameless Nevada mine.

The beam of the flashlight showed the same gray tunnel with each new curve and turn. It began to feel like he was going nowhere fast when he realized a sound in the dark that he had not noticed previously.

Voices, barely audible, whispered in the dark. They were not close or pursuing but coming from above. Voices from the ceiling.

Shane raised the flashlight and scanned the rock. Holes, some barely noticeable and others as large as a fist, pocked the surface. They were places where stone had broken free, maybe flaked loose during the tunneling process and finally shaken free during the rumblings created by the enraged Burners.

Nothing offered Shane a potential escape; he doubted he could have even fit an arm through the holes he saw. But he was being watched through them.

The ghosts from the mine above, the disfigured spirits that had chosen not to speak on their initial meeting, peered at him through the holes and cracks. Some were obscured almost entirely, with only an eye visible. He saw others more clearly, half a face here or a pair of eyes fixed on him as he passed.

They spoke in hushed tones, words he could not make out. Their whispers were for each other, not for Shane, but they watched him closely as he passed. Over the murmuring of the spirits above, another sound filled the tunnel from back the way he had come. It was sudden and harsh, a shriek that broadened into almost a roar. Something bestial.

Lights flickered and reflected off the wall behind Shane, white and brighter than any flashlight. One of the Burners had descended into the tunnel after him. The ground shook, and a beam of light bounced from one tunnel wall to the next, fracturing and diffusing in an irregular kaleidoscope of patterns off the uneven surface.

The tunnel glowed, and Shane began to run. The Burner was not close enough to see him yet: The zigzagging path that had been chewed through the rock kept him ahead of his pursuer but just barely. The light was also not strong enough to cause any harm yet. It was too dim and carried no heat by the time it reached him, but it still illuminated his way. It would not be long before the Burner was close enough to attack, and there was no cover in the tunnel.

Shane had no choice but to run. The whispers above him grew louder and more intense as he did so. Some laughed, and he made out words here and there. They were mocking him.

"...never escape..."

"...die down there..."

He initially thought they were talking to him, but they were telling one another what they thought would happen, or what they hoped would happen. None of it was for him. They still didn't care enough to speak directly to him.

"The Waste will get him first," one said, and the statement brought silence for a split second as though the proclamation was deeply profound and required reflection.

"The Waste is gone," another said, and for the first time, it seemed like the spirits were not seeking to disturb him with their words or making ominous threats at his expense.

"The Waste is never far."

Their murmuring increased, a frenzied debate not about if Shane would die or be lost in the darkness and rot forever in the cave. Now they spoke of whatever the Waste was and if it was coming back. They sounded afraid.

Though a Burner was giving chase in the tunnel, Shane did not believe it was the Waste the ghosts were worried about. They meant the same thing that had occupied his thoughts. The thing that had dug the tunnel and perhaps left that fused monstrosity in its wake had left many ghosts in the mine terrified of its presence.

"He'll see soon," one of the ghosts above him said.

"Almost there," one teased, and for the first time, Shane felt like he was being addressed directly.

"Run faster," another said, and the tone was laced with sarcasm.

Shane gripped the flashlight tightly and took another bend in the tunnel, distancing himself from the Burner but also heading back in almost the same direction he had just come. He needed an opening, a way out, instead of the endless back-and-forth tunneling. If even one of the holes in the cave ceiling was large enough to get an arm through, maybe he could pull more of the rock down and create an escape. He could use the grooves in the walls as footholds and climb if he had to.

The Burner shrieked again, and rock tumbled from the ceiling. The whispers became shouts, and the ghosts were talking over one another. It became hard to make out anything being said, but Shane ignored them all as he ran, taking another sharp curve in the tunnel, and coming to an abrupt halt.

Some of the shouts were replaced by laughter, and it spread. The path ahead of Shane had caved in. There was a chasm in the rock, a split that delved deep into the earth. Shane stood at the precipice and shone the light down. The bottom was beyond its reach.

The ceiling above was as thin as it had been anywhere. A massive chunk of stone had fallen free whenever the floor had cracked and been swallowed up below. The far side of the chasm was peppered with stones large enough to be small boulders, but none had broken enough of the ceiling loose to make an escape. It would be too precarious to even try with the chasm below him, anyway.

Shane grunted and kicked a small rock over the edge. He watched it fall for a split second in the beam of the flashlight, and then it vanished. A second passed, and then another and another. He heard nothing over the laughter of the ghosts above him. If the rock found bottom, it was too far away and too quiet for him to hear.

The distance from one side to the other was not immense. Shane's leg still ached, but the gap was not insurmountable. He had no time to debate the issue. Even if he stayed and fought the Burner, even if he defeated it, then what? He still needed to be on the other side of the chasm.

Shane stepped back from the ledge until he was at the wall of the curve that led toward it. The mocking ghosts had quieted, aware of what he was doing. Some debated his chances; others predicted his doom. He clenched his jaw and ran.

The ground was uneven, and the wound in his leg throbbed but he pushed, keeping the light directed down so he could see where he needed to jump. He reached the edge and pushed off with his good leg, lunging forward across the gap. The ghosts stopped as one, and the tunnel went deathly silent until he hit the far side with a thud.

Shane grunted when his chest hit the far ledge. The flashlight clattered across the tunnel floor away from him, and he grasped at the rock, his legs and torso dangling over the edge and into the darkness.

He used his boots to scrape and push as he clawed forward, gripping the irregularities in the stone and pulling up until he felt rock under his legs. The light went out, and Shane was plunged into darkness.

"It's too late."

The voice was closer than any of the other whispers. Shane lifted his head and looked around, but he could see nothing. He crawled forward to where he remembered the flashlight being and patted around on the tunnel floor but felt no sign of it.

Shane reached into his pocket and retrieved his lighter, sparking it to life before getting to his feet. The flashlight had vanished, likely down the chasm with the rock that he had kicked.

Across the gap, the flickering light of the flame cast moving shadows across the rough-hewn surface of the wall. A figure appeared from the dark, shadows dancing across its almost featureless face. The flesh had melted like wax, covering its eyes and dripping from its nose and chin.

The drooping lips parted, exposing stained teeth the color of wood, and the ghost screamed.

The world shook as though it were ending.

CHAPTER 20

THE WASTE

Light burst from all over the Burner's body. Shane stumbled back, turning and swiftly taking cover behind one of the small boulder-sized rocks as the blinding light filled the tunnel and the shriek shook the walls and floor.

Rock slabs fell and shattered around him. The ghosts in the mine had fallen silent or fled, leaving Shane and the Burner alone. Only the chasm separated them now, and it would not be an issue for the spirit to cross.

He waited as the light grew in intensity, making his body as small as he could while the temperature in the tunnel rose to a nearly unbearable level. Hidden though he was, he still felt it searing his skin and penetrating his clothing like he was in an oven.

If Shane had caught the ghost by surprise, he might have had a chance. But now, his only chance was to run, and he could only run if it went dim.

Sweat rolled down his back as Shane remained huddled behind the rock. It was only seconds, but time felt like it was moving impossibly slowly. Finally, the light faded and the heat subsided. He got to his feet, ready to flee, when a second Burner blazed to life next to the first.

The new ghost's head was free of skin or muscle, just a glowing skull atop a burned and scarred body. It screamed as soon as Shane stood, and the tunnel crumbled again, forcing him to the ground to avoid more falling rocks and another blast of searing light.

Stones pelted Shane, some from above and some as shrapnel when larger chunks hit the ground and broke apart. He could not risk looking up at the blinding light, so he had no idea when new chunks were falling or where.

As the second blast of light faded, the earth continued to shake more violently than before. The boulder Shane was hidden behind shifted, and he got to his knees, still staying low and as out of sight as he could.

Neither of the Burners was making noise, but the rumbling was growing stronger. They had triggered something in the earth, maybe they had weakened the chasm, and the tunnel was shaking as though the ground was going to swallow it whole.

There was nowhere for Shane to run where the Burners could not reach him, but he'd be crushed if he stayed. He cursed as a huge slab of stone fell to the ground behind him, shattering and peppering his back with shrapnel. The stone set off a cascade as the entire tunnel caved in, sealing off the way ahead as more rubble piled in.

Light began to build again. Shane saw it creeping up the walls. He stayed low, crouched behind the boulder, thinking of a way to proceed that wouldn't end with him buried alive or burned to a cinder.

The rumbling increased, and he stood. He had to double back; it was his only option. Fight past the Burners and get back to the way he'd come in.

The Burners were not glowing. They stood across the gap, backing away as a rich, yellow-orange light like fire rose from deep in the earth. They were not casting the light: Something was rising from the depths, awoken by their presence.

The tunnel collapsed behind him, and a rush of fresh air came down with it. Shane could barely see in the light of whatever was rising from below, but the tunnel above, the mine itself, was exposed again. The collapse had opened the ceiling.

Shane growled deep in his chest and shook his head. He ran at the pile of rubble, putting the Burners behind him. He leaped onto the rocks and began to climb. The most unstable slabs slipped away under his weight, falling to one side or another, but he pressed on.

He moved swiftly, holding the larger stones when he could, even as the shakes became violent enough that he could barely maintain his footing. His fear was that the tunnel above and the mine itself would collapse next.

One of the Burners wailed, and the bright light pierced the darkness. It was a controlled burst, a directed beam of light, not at Shane but down into the chasm. Shane turned to look back, squinting against the light, and watched as something from the gap wreathed in a yellow glow reached up and grabbed the Burner by the leg.

The white light flickered and went dead as the ghost cried out, not in rage but surprise. Next to it, the second Burner flashed white as the first was pulled down. Shane could not see what it was through the blinding light, only that something had taken hold of the ghost and dragged it below.

His curiosity was not stronger than his survival instinct. Shane climbed, pushing through fallen rock until his hand felt something cold and solid, an old mine cart track, and he used it to brace himself as he pulled himself out of the lower tunnel and then kept running.

The Burner below screeched, and another flash of light filled the tunnel behind him. He did not pause to look over his shoulder, he just ran.

He could not even hear his footfalls in the darkness. There was only the fierce shaking and the sounds of falling rocks. No deformed ghosts barred his path. They had vanished with the appearance of whatever had crept up from the depths.

Images flashed in Shane's mind, shadows cast in the blinding lights from the Burners. He had seen a shape, nothing more. An appendage from the depths, large and dexterous. It grabbed the Burner's leg firmly and dragged it down. But it had been so hard to see in the piercing light. An arm, a dozen arms, something else altogether, he didn't know. But it had no fear of the Burners, and the scorching light they wielded had not slowed down whatever it was.

The shaking diminished only briefly as Shane ran along the tunnel.

The Burner he'd left behind cried out again, and the rumbling increased. Shane followed the tracks on the ground, and the tunnel sloped up and gave way to a room.

A cage and an elevator sat framed in wood at the bottom of a shaft. Shane ran toward it, climbing up a wooden ladder that had been fixed to the wall alongside the ancient elevator. Above him was a dark sky. He could make out stars, but they were high above.

One of the ghosts from the mine, its face twisted with burns and malformed flesh, clutched the wooden ladder several feet above him. It looked like it had been trying to escape and then lost its nerve part way up.

Whatever the ghost's intentions, it was in Shane's way. He grabbed at its leg and pulled it off the ladder, trying to throw it to the ground below. It clutched at some of the other wooden framework and held itself up as Shane continued his climb.

"Please," the ghost said gruffly as Shane passed. It reached for him, grabbing at his arm. "Please help me."

"Help yourself." He shrugged off its grip and continued to climb. The shaft was shaking. Dust and stones were falling, and the odd wooden plank came with it. As whatever crawled up from the earth got closer, the shaft was bound to collapse.

"I can't... I can't leave," the ghost said. "It's been too long."

Shane continued his climb and the ghost paced him, its twisted face a mask of desperation and panic.

"You look like you're doing fine," Shane told the spirit.

It shook its head and looked down.

"We're not supposed to leave. Ever." Its voice cracked.

"So stay," Shane said.

The ghost whined almost childishly and began to climb again.

"We can't stay. No one can stay anymore."

"What's coming out of that hole?" Shane asked.

He was moving as quickly as he could, hand over hand, climbing the ladder out of the shaft even as the wound in his leg screamed. Some of the planks were missing and some were loose, but he pressed on. The spirit paced him, begging for some sort of non-specific help.

"It's the Waste," the ghost said, climbing at Shane's side. "They woke it up again!"

"Who did?" Shane asked.

"The Burners. Their godforsaken shrieking. They knew it was down here somewhere. Everyone knows it's down here, and they did it anyway, all to catch you and your friends."

Shane was breathing heavily. The mine shaft was long, and getting to the top was taking all the energy he had. Below him, the flickering yellow and orange light had caught up with them. The Waste, whatever it was, was coming.

"You saw my friends?"

"They got out. They went this way. But it won't matter if we can't get away from it."

"And what the hell are we getting away from? What is the Waste?"

"I don't know," the ghost whispered. "No one knows what it is. But it eats everything. It'll devour me, same as you. We have to get away!"

Shane didn't understand what the ghost expected. It was climbing fine, it didn't need him, and it surely didn't expect him to fight the Waste.

"You're getting away. Keep climbing." Shane hoped to get through whatever mental block seemed to be making the ghost think it couldn't free itself.

"You don't understand," the ghost cried, shaking his head. "You don't understand!"

Shane continued climbing, and the ghost stopped. Its arms reached feebly for the next bit of frame, the next handhold that was well within its grasp, but it was like an unseen chain had been wrapped around the spirit's wrist and prevented its arm from fully extending.

"Please!" the ghost begged. "Please help me!"

Shane realized what the problem was. The ghost had reached the end of its range. It had traveled a mile from whatever haunted item had bound it to the earth. It could not escape through the mine shaft. It would go no farther.

"You have to go back," Shane told it. "Hide in the rock. Double back the way you came and escape somewhere else."

"It won't work. Nothing gets past the Waste. Nothing gets away."

He kept climbing, leaving the ghost behind as it cried out for him, begging him to do the impossible by taking it with him. It could stay where it was or it could go back; there was nothing else.

"Hide," Shane shouted down to the ghost.

He didn't know why he bothered. The ghost and its companions had been more than happy at the prospect of his death not so long ago. Now that it was in trouble, its attitude had drastically changed.

"You can't hide from Death," the ghost yelled at him. "It'll find you, too. You won't get away!"

The mine shaft seemed to shift, and a slide of rock ran down the side at Shane's back, dragging much of the elevator framework with it. The ghost fell, and the light below rolled and twisted like an inferno. Shane saw a shape, a mass in the fire, but he was too far up to make anything out clearly, and it seemed to only be partially there, struggling to drag down the entire structure.

Hand over hand, Shane raced to the top. The rocks collapsed and wooden framing rained on his head. The night sky was clear above him, so close now, as long as the shaft held.

Ladder planks pulled off the wall under his weight as the rock slid away. Shane pushed off and jumped for the next one above his head, clutching the edges with his fingers as he kicked off bare rock to get his footing. He used his arms to pull himself up to the next step, and then the next.

The wood of the final ladder plank was gritty from the desert sand,

and he gripped it tightly. It shifted under his weight, pulling free on the left side as it rotated and then popped loose on the right.

Shane felt himself falling back, with nothing under his feet to support his weight and a useless piece of wood in his hands.

Chapter 21

Surfacing

Shane fell, but only for a moment. A cool, firm hand clasped over his wrist, and his body jerked. He bounced off the stone wall and looked up into Coulson's smiling face.

"You make everything so dramatic," the ghost said, hauling him out of the hole.

The wooden frame for the elevator splintered above their heads and the top section, set with a massive gear and cables, fell free.

Coulson pulled Shane away from the framework as it collapsed, fracturing into pieces as it fell into the mineshaft. The hole expanded, with more rock flaking off and tumbling down the hole as the man and the ghost ran from the entrance and up a small ridge.

Dust rose into the night in a great cloud as the rumbling subsided. The mineshaft had collapsed, swallowed up by the earth, but the violent shaking from below had ended. The Waste had moved on or gone quiet.

Ventura waited a few yards away, the iron baton in his hand, watching as Shane came back.

"What the hell was that?" the FBI agent asked, still watching the huge dust cloud rising in the darkness.

"They call it the Waste," Shane said. "It's big and angry."

"Waste?" Coulson asked.

"I never saw it, but I think it carved an entire tunnel with its bare hands. It eats the dead, and it's probably what took the bodies in Doomtown. The ghosts down there were terrified of it," Shane said.

He paused, catching his breath and leaning against a tree while he adjusted the bandage on his leg.

"What happened with you two?" he asked.

"Ran a lot. Fought some ghosts. Met a hunchback," Coulson explained.

"Really?" Shane took a cigarette from his pocket and lit it.

"It was a ghost. Russian, badly disfigured. He had control over the Burners. We were going to leave this place in case he came back, but we only got a hundred yards or so when the ground started shaking. Something was moving toward the mineshaft, so we doubled back to see what was happening," Ventura said.

"Glad you did," Shane said.

"Yeah. Glad to see you made it." Ventura clapped him on the shoulder.

Shane looked back at the hole in the ground. The dust was settling, and the earth was still. The Waste was not coming up, but if it was tunneling anywhere, it had learned to do it quietly. He suspected it had not gone far. If that was the case, he was happy to put in the effort on his behalf.

"We should go," he said. "In case your hunchback or whatever was after me comes back. It dragged two Burners into the ground. It's not something we want to square off with."

"We were going to take cover over there." Ventura pointed to some hills in the near distance.

The ground rumbled underfoot again, and Shane had to grab the tree to stay upright. There was no easing into it like a slowly building earthquake. Instead, the desert shook violently as something moved very distinctly east underfoot. It was the Waste, tunneling again, digging toward something and leaving the mine behind.

Coulson turned his back on Shane and Ventura, following the path of the thundering thing beneath the ground, but stopped after only a few paces as though watching a car pull out and drive off without him.

"You got something?" Shane asked.

Coulson shook his head.

"Not a damn thing." He almost sounded surprised. "I tried to see it. Tried to form an image in my mind, and it pushed back at me."

Shane looked at Ventura, and the other man shrugged.

"So, that's not normal?" Shane asked.

Coulson turned around to face them again.

"The only time that ever happened to me before was with Jillian, and we were just goofing around. Her power is not quite the same as mine, but she could push me back, stop me from seeing into her mind. This thing stopped me from seeing it at all. It was like trying to see people inside a house by looking at the brick wall outside."

"So how would something go about doing that? It's obviously rare, right? What does it mean?" Ventura asked.

"It means… you need to have power like mine to do that. The amount of psychic energy, just pure power of your mind, must be well beyond anything I've encountered in any other living thing. Or dead thing."

Shane thought of the spirit he had fought in the cavern. Three heads, merged, and part of one ghost. All had to be destroyed before the thing was defeated.

"Okay, so what if it was a lot of minds together?" he asked.

"No," Coulson said. "It's one entity. One being, I just can't… see it. I can't get a glimpse."

"I'm not saying it's more than one thing. But what if that one thing has more than one mind?"

The ember in Coulson's cigarette flared brightly, and he narrowed his eyes.

"What did you see down there?"

"A ghost," Shane said. "Made up of three bodies. Fused together down to the bone. One body, but the pieces of all of them together. I destroyed it, but it took three tries to put it down."

Coulson stared at him for a moment as though weighing his words, and then he looked back east, the way the rumbling had gone.

"Three minds couldn't—"

"More than three." Shane cut him off. "What if it's a lot more than three?"

"How many?" Ventura asked.

Shane shook his head.

"Like I said, I didn't see it. But the tunnel down there was huge. What if it was dozens? Dozens and dozens of minds and bodies fused together to make one thing with many minds?"

Ventura laughed a quick bark of incredulity.

"Come on," he said with little conviction. "That can't happen. How could it?"

"I don't know," Shane said. "But the ghost I fought was guarding its body. The bones were merged, bonded. They had grown together to become one thing. The third head was inside the ribcage of one of the others. It wasn't just the ghost, it was the living people that became the ghost."

"And they call it the Waste?" Coulson said.

"The ghosts in the mine did. They said it ate everything. Sound familiar?" Shane said.

Coulson nodded. The Doomtown spirits had told him the same thing. Something below the ground was after them and eating everything. It had consumed the spirits there, and their physical remains, and had swallowed at least two Burners below the mine. Now, it was off toward whatever waited east. The place where they suspected the PULSE lab waited for them.

"So, our mystery monster is a ghost, but it's also many ghosts. One and many at the same time," Ventura said. "What does that mean for us?"

"Means it's going to be hard as hell to fight if every part needs to be destroyed to get rid of the whole," Shane said.

"Yeah," Coulson said. "Going to be an interesting fight."

Shane wondered what the ghost meant by that. If the Waste was resisting his ability to even see it, what would it do if he fought it? Coulson's fists were not real; he wasn't fighting like Shane was. All his power was the same as far as Shane knew. But he didn't doubt that Coulson had more tricks up his sleeve than he had shown. He didn't seem like the kind of guy who would lay it all out on the table, even with someone he trusted.

"So, this thing is on the run," Shane said. "Not in fear, but it's got a plan. And your hunchback is out here with a team of Burners looking to go scorched earth. What do you want to do?"

He knew what *he* wanted to do next, but he wasn't a ranking officer, and this was no military campaign. They needed to work as a team or none of them would make it out of the desert.

"We go," Ventura said. "Right? We hunt them before they can hunt us."

Coulson laughed.

"I don't need sleep; you don't need to ask me. Let's go," he said.

Shane hadn't doubted that Coulson was willing to run headlong into danger. He was surprised Ventura took to it so easily, though. And glad. He wanted to track the Waste while they could still follow it. And if they ran into some stray Burners in the desert along the way to wherever it was going, so be it. It would leave their hunchback with less backup if they could take out one or two.

The trio headed east, following the rumbling path of the unseen monster beneath the sand. If it was heading for the PULSE lab, maybe it was already going after the same thing they were.

Ventura had not brought it up yet, but it must have crossed Coulson's mind that letting the Waste get to the lab and letting it attack and devour more Burners was probably a bad idea. If it was gaining strength from the things it devoured, the Burners would be an exceptional power boost.

"How far do you think we are from Doomtown?" Ventura asked as they walked, Coulson still serving as their guide.

"A few miles," Shane guessed. Their passage through the mine had given his sense of direction and distance a run for its money. In the dark, with no frame of reference, it was impossible to tell for sure how far they'd gone.

"How far can this Waste travel?" Ventura asked.

Shane grunted, considering the question. It had raided Doomtown and now was tunneling east. The lab could have been miles ahead. The Waste was breaking the rules. Unless, of course, it wasn't.

"The Waste might be one entity made of many," Shane said, throwing a lot of faith into speculation. "If each ghost is an individual but also a piece of the whole, it's like a beehive."

"Ghost honey for everyone." Coulson flicked the ash from his cigarette.

"So, maybe each ghost is still bound by the distance limitation individually, but the whole supersedes that," Shane suggested.

"How?" Ventura asked.

"It gets its mile from everyone. Ten ghosts fused into one with ten haunted items each a mile apart, the Waste gets a ten-mile range out of it."

"Is that possible?" Ventura asked.

Shane shrugged, looking up at the stars.

"What is and is not possible is not my area of expertise, and I have learned that weighing in on it gets you nowhere," he replied.

"Probably best just to agree that this thing is weird and dangerous," Coulson said. "Getting bogged down in the details of the thing that might eat you later tonight won't help."

"Fair enough," Ventura said.

They passed through a small valley full of dry grass and an abundance of twisted little trees before coming out on a dune that overlooked a dry riverbed full of rocks. Coulson stopped them at the top, signaling for the others to get down.

Shane dropped quickly, crawling to the edge of the dune's peak and looking down at what awaited them. A single ghost, thin and small, walked slowly and stiffly through the rocks of the riverbed. Pale flesh clung tight to its bones, and it reminded him of Eloise in an odd way.

"One of the Burners that came at us before," Coulson said softly. He scanned the riverbed. "I don't see the others."

Shane would have considered letting it go before, hiding until it passed, but if the Waste sought to feed on them, to grow stronger, it was not a good idea to leave one around. Besides, if the hunchback was commanding them and wanted them to kill the three of them, they'd be killing two birds with one stone by getting rid of it. If he could get the drop on it.

"Wait here," Shane whispered.

"What are you going to do?" Ventura asked.

"I'm going to burn that Burner," he answered before heading south along the dune to the riverbed.

CHAPTER 22

BURNED

The ghost's eyes were sealed. The dried flesh was puckered where the lids came together and sealed with a crusty layer of brownish goo. Its movements were careful but still awkward and uncoordinated. It weaved through the dry, smooth rocks of the old riverbed, heading southwest at a slow but steady pace.

The river curved to the right, toward the end of a sand dune and thicket of trees and scrub grass that grew there like a tiny oasis. The ghost shambled past, paying them no heed.

Two steps past a midsized Joshua tree, it finally turned its head, too late to do anything as Shane emerged from his hiding place and grabbed the ghost from behind. His right arm circled the ghost's throat while he reached across its face with his left and twisted.

The ghost's neck snapped. Shane dragged it to the ground, laying it out quickly on the flat stones. His attack had been as smooth as possible, quick, and efficient. The Burner only began to glow after it was on its back with Shane kneeling on top of it.

Shriveled, dark lips parted to produce a scream. Shane's hands were on either side of its smooth, waxy skull, and he squeezed and pushed down at the same time. The ghost's head shattered like glass, and the body burst, knocking Shane back toward the dune. He landed in sand, a gentle fall all things considered, and sat up quickly.

Coulson and Ventura appeared over the dune, with Coulson offering a slow clap of approval.

"Very clean. Just need to do that a dozen more times or whatever it is, and we're golden."

"No problem." Shane took a deep breath before getting to his feet.

Destroying the Burners was doable. The right opportunity had fallen into his lap. Still, if they could hunt the ghosts and control the setting, they had a chance. It might not get them closer to the PULSE lab and the Waste, but it would solve at least one problem.

They headed east again after Shane took a moment to catch his breath and adjust the bandage on his leg. Coulson could not hear the Waste any longer to know where it had gone, but they stayed on the same bearing it had been on.

Within several minutes, they had drifted close to another of the bunkers. Coulson saw it first, his eyes better suited to seeing in the dark than those of a living man. Two Burners were there, standing idly in the sand as though lost and confused.

"Can we handle two?" Ventura asked.

The three men were on their stomachs, watching the bunker from a distance, and waiting to see if the Burners did anything when idle. They seemed to be turned off and zombie-like.

"These two are Burnt Souls," Coulson said. "The Burners are smarter. These guys are just reactive. I think we can take them."

"We need to distract them," Ventura said. "Something to get their attention so you two can get the drop on them and take them out quickly."

"Ideally," Coulson said. "You volunteering?"

He meant it as a joke, but Ventura shrugged.

"Yeah, I guess. I can't destroy them. Might as well make myself useful."

"You sure?" Shane wasn't about to tell the man not to risk his life, but he wanted to make sure Ventura was up to the task.

"Yeah. I'll circle the bunker and draw their attention to it while staying out of sight. Maybe they won't spark up if they can't see me. Should give you guys a minute to sneak up on them."

"Take them at the same time, and no one has to go Fourth of July," Shane said.

"Watch your back, Agent," Coulson said.

Ventura took a moment, staring across the dark sands at the outlines of the Burnt Souls and the concrete bunker, and then nodded as though listening to an unheard voice. He broke to the right and circled wide, staying low among the rocks and scrub and small dunes where he couldn't be seen.

Shane and Coulson edged closer, using the landscape to stay out of sight as well. The Burnt Souls seemed like robots that had been shut down and left out. They were still and silent, their burned bodies like corpses propped up as decorations.

Coulson split ways with Shane to get closer to the second spirit, saying nothing and creeping soundlessly. As a ghost, he had the benefit of not making noise. Shane was forced to be more cautious and got as close as he dared to the nearest of the spirits before stopping behind a rock bordered by scrub grass.

The minutes ticked by, and Shane had seen no sign of Ventura since he'd left them. The two Burnt Souls showed no sign they'd been alerted to anything until a loud banging drew their attention. The sound of something hitting hard against steel echoed across the dark desert. Someone was banging on the bunker door, on the far side of the concrete wall.

The Burnt Souls moved as one, turning and stumbling toward the bunker. Shane was on his feet the instant the ghost's back was turned, as was Coulson. They moved in sync, each taking a ghost from behind at almost the same moment.

Shane dragged his ghost to the ground while Coulson lifted his by its head, crushing it in his hands within seconds. The one Shane had taken down began to glow ominously across its body. He drove his elbow into the ghost's face twice, breaking its nose and orbital bone before putting pressure with his palms on the already broken face.

The glow was just becoming too bright to look at when the spirit's head buckled. The blast rolled him backward in time to watch Ventura running from the side of the bunker toward them, his arms pumping while his legs covered incredibly long strides.

"One more!" he yelled, coming for the two of them.

A third ghost, this one a Burner, crept around the corner of the bunker wall and raised a hand that was as bright as the sun. The light swept in a powerful beam across the desert sand, scorching the plants, and melting sand to glass. Smoke rose in acrid, black plumes, and a smell like burning metal filled the air.

Shane rolled behind a rock, and Ventura ducked for cover as well. Only Coulson remained, out of sight of the Burner with his back to the bunker wall. He waited for the spirit to step into view and thrust his hand toward the ghost. It was not a fist, but his hand with fingers outstretched. Ghost flesh passed through ghost flesh, and his hand was inside the Burner's head. A moment later, the ghost's head exploded, and the ghost went with it.

The force knocked Coulson against the concrete bunker so powerfully that the wall broke. Coulson slumped to the ground, his back still to the wall and his legs spread out before him like he was tired and just needed to sit. Ventura reached him first while Shane was a few steps behind.

"That would have killed you," Ventura said to Shane, touching the broken bunker wall.

Shane didn't reply, but Ventura was probably not wrong. Burners exploded harder when they were charged. It seemed that the excess energy had to go somewhere. It was nearly enough power to launch Coulson through a wall, so it probably would have at least broken Shane's ribs if not his back.

"Yeah, that was rough," Coulson agreed. "Better scouting next time."

"Next time," Ventura said with a laugh. "Right."

Coulson took a moment before getting to his feet. Shane made eye contact with the ghost but neither said anything. He was a dead man and didn't need to rest before getting up after being knocked down. He shouldn't have, anyway. The fights were taking their toll on him.

Shane hoped Coulson knew his limitations, but he also understood enough about the ghost's motivations to doubt whether he'd pay attention to them. Coulson would destroy himself if he thought it was important enough. He wouldn't make a big deal out of it, either. He'd do it without saying a word, which meant Shane had to keep his eyes open. If it happened, he wouldn't have long to catch it and do anything about it.

They continued east. The layout of the bunkers seemed to be in a horseshoe pattern, as they discovered another that was a mile and a half past the first. This one was monitored by a single Burner. Shane snuck up on it with Ventura serving as a distraction.

The Burner's destruction was swift. Once again, it was barely able to ignite its powers before Shane took it out. Nothing else was inside the bunker, and there was no sign of any companions.

Another mile of travel, and Coulson saw something new on the horizon. Instead of a small, concrete bunker monitored by ghost guards, they approached a security fence. Like the one that bordered the entire site, this one was lined with razor wire but lacked military guards.

Like the bunkers, it looked to have been built in what was otherwise the middle of nowhere. No road led up to it, and the landscape was just rocks, sand, and scrub. Shane could identify nothing notable about the place other than the fact it was isolated. This far into the desert behind a security fence, it was not the sort of place anyone was likely to discover by accident. You either had to know where to go or at the very least follow an unseen monstrosity burrowing through the stone beneath the ground.

The trio approached cautiously. The darkness offered them some cover, but Shane knew a ghost could see him far more easily than he could see them. They used the desert for cover, keeping low and moving behind trees and rocks, closing in on the facility slowly but carefully.

There were no lights and no signs of movement as they approached. Beyond the fence was another facility, this one much larger than the bunkers that served as homes for the Burners.

Even from a distance in the dark, Shane saw something was wrong with the doors of the facility. Set into the concrete wall, they were two large, steel, blast doors. They would normally have been large enough to open and let military vehicles pass through, far bigger than those of the bunkers in the desert. But the metal had been melted from the center out.

Molten steel had poured from the doors and solidified again in dark, flowing bulges. It looked like candle wax in the dark. Something extremely powerful, and extremely hot, had forced its way out from the inside.

"This has to be the lab," Ventura said. "Right? What else could it be?"

Like the bunkers, it looked like the bulk of the structure was underground. The concrete aboveground was wide but not high. It was impossible to see what was beyond the doors, at least in the dark, but Shane suspected it was an elevator.

There were no signs on the lab, and no markings to indicate what it was or who ran it. The fence was melted through in more than one spot, rendering the chained and padlocked gate useless. Everything about it screamed abandoned despite Coulson's earlier assurances that someone was still working there.

"We need to get inside," Ventura said.

"Yeah," Coulson agreed, "but it's not going to be easy."

He pointed to the northern side of the facility. Shane saw nothing at first in the darkness until finally, after a moment, he saw movement. A single ghost, maybe a Burnt Soul, shuffled a few paces and then stopped again.

Shane soon realized that more of them were standing there. Once he knew what to look for, he saw at least a dozen of them standing along the front of the facility at random intervals, some swaying gently and others moving a step or two in one direction before going back in the other.

Another spirit appeared from the entrance. This one walked casually with typical, unencumbered strides. Shane could not make out the details of the face or the body, but it walked like anyone out for a stroll in the night, doing a quick circuit of the area, ignoring the other ghosts, and then heading back inside.

"Burners." Ventura crouched lower and indicated a spot to the south.

Three of the ghosts approached in the dark, passing through one of the melted holes in the fence. They made their way to the front entrance as well and headed inside.

"What's your count?" Shane asked.

"Sixteen so far," Coulson said. "Four Burners for sure. These ones out front are weird, though. Not sure they're even Burnt Souls if that matters. Still, a hell of a lot of dead guys."

"I don't think I can distract sixteen," Ventura said.

Shane said nothing and continued to observe. They would never be able to distract sixteen, but it didn't matter. They couldn't fight that many, either.

They needed a new plan.

CHAPTER 23
INTO THE FIRE

Shane crept between rocks, choosing his footing carefully so as to not make too much noise and draw attention to himself. Coulson had taken point ahead of him and was drifting across the sand without touching it, creeping like fog toward the fence.

Ventura was in the rear. He was less used to stealth travel than the other two but still managed to keep the sound he made to a minimum. It would not be too hard to keep out of sight of the ghosts outside of the facility, but if they heard something coming for them, all their efforts to remain unseen would be for nothing.

Coulson made it to the edge of the fence. He was only a few feet from a hole that had been melted through the chain link, but he paused there to scout the area again, looking over the assorted ghosts that wandered out front.

The ground began to vibrate, and Coulson looked back at the other two. No one moved, but the vibrations increased.

The Burners from inside the facility came back outside. The slower and more confused-looking spirits were agitated, and they bumbled around, but Coulson was right. They were not the same as the Burnt Souls they had fought. Those, aimless as they might have been, seemed to have more control. The ones outside the facility seemed more like confused animals.

Ghosts wandered haphazardly, some of them moaning softly, as the four Burners proceeded to the fence line. The first of them raised a hand, and a bright light scorched the night. Shane winced and averted his eyes as the Burner melted a new segment of fence yards from him and the others. The other Burners followed the first one past the fence into the desert as the rumbling increased.

The feeling was powerful enough that it traveled through the ground and into the rocks and trees. Shane felt himself shaking. Sand spilled down the sides of dunes and rolled off rocks.

One of the Burners ignited and directed a blast of searing white energy straight into the ground. The sand glowed even brighter as it melted, and bits of sediment and other particles smoked, creating a chemical, burning smell that carried on the night breeze.

A chasm formed under the Burner, and it fell back, the beam of white light twisting into the night and arcing across the sky before going out. A second Burner took up the attack, and a great, echoing bellow rose from the ground as yellow fire surged through the collapsing sands.

"No!" someone yelled, barely audible over the chaos unfolding in the desert.

Shane turned to the facility and saw a hunched-over ghost with a massive growth on his back, the hunchback Coulson and Ventura told him about, running through the melted doors.

"This side of the fence! This side!" the ghost shouted, his words lost in the rumbling outside.

Something shadowy, hidden behind the flames and plumes of dust, rose from the ground and pulled two of the Burners below. Shane tried to see what it was, but it moved quickly, dragging the ghosts away like a snake striking at prey.

"It's going to take them all," Shane said.

"Good riddance," Ventura whispered. "One less chance for us to die."

"Except it's feeding on them. And they're powered up," Shane said. As Coulson had demonstrated by nearly going through a concrete wall, when they were powered up, they had a lot of energy to spare. And now, the Waste was taking it.

The other two Burners tried to retreat, but the chasm in the desert floor had grown too large. Sand sucked into it from all sides like a massive sinkhole, and only the yellow flames escaped.

The third Burner was pulled in with flames licking at its back. The fourth made it to the fence line and crossed over. Shane could see the edges of metal plates beneath the earth as the sand receded. The fence was the surface barrier, but someone had built an iron wall around the facility below. Someone had been prepared well in advance.

Coulson waved Shane and Ventura over. With everyone else distracted by the Waste, it was their best shot at accessing the facility. They passed through the melted fence and onto the grounds, remaining out of sight as they made a beeline for the closest wall of the facility. It was the only cover available, but they were exposed on the path toward it.

Shane and Ventura ran while Coulson drifted soundlessly. A twitching, partially disfigured ghost with its arms wrapped around itself jerked as the ground shook beneath everyone's feet and turned toward them. One single, brown eye locked on Shane, and the ghost's mouth, half-sealed with melted flesh, parted in a scream.

Shane wondered how long the iron in the ground would protect them from the Waste, or, more specifically, how deep the wall went. It would not be long before the entity realized it could go over or under the barrier. But it would not happen soon enough to be a helpful distraction.

The ghost began to strobe, a light flashing within its chest that never fully ignited. Coulson was right: These things were not Burners or even Burnt Souls but some lesser thing like a failed version of the others that couldn't quite control whatever power had been imbued in it. Nevertheless, the light that strobed from its body was still blinding and gave off random bursts of heat. It was unpredictable and dangerous, and its shrieks drew the attention of the others.

"No no no!" the hunchback ghost yelled. "Stop them! Kill them now!"

The other twisted and unstable guards were all focused on them now, as was the final Burner that had survived the Waste. Outside the fence, the ground still churned and rumbled, but the wall buried in the earth prevented it from getting closer.

More ghosts lit up, each as inconsistent as the others. Some only produced a dim glow; others had fractures in their flesh from which light escaped, or it was localized to their hands or heads. None seemed to have control over it, but they all shambled together like a crowd of zombies toward Shane and the others.

Behind them, the surviving Burner locked eyes with Shane. The ghost still had most of its face though a severe burn from torso to chin had eaten away its flesh down to the bone. The rest was untouched and glowed white in the slowly brightening light. Dark eyes looked into Shane's as a smile crossed the ghost's lips.

There was no cover for them, and nowhere to duck out of the way of what was coming. They were too far from the facility entrance, and the nearest rocks were back the way they had come.

Ventura had already pulled out his iron baton, ready to fight as he moved back to avoid random bursts of heat and light from the broken ghosts.

The Burner's body burst to life with no buildup. It was blazing white in the blink of an eye, causing Shane to raise his hand and turn away. He saw Ventura do the same, wincing as he stumbled and shielded his eyes. Only Coulson stayed facing forward.

"We have to get out of here," Ventura said.

"There's nowhere to go." Coulson put a hand on Ventura's shoulder to steady him. "You got one more run in you?"

"What?"

"Distract them. Draw them together toward the door. I'll do what I can."

"Coulson…" Ventura began.

The heat from the Burner was growing, but it moved like it had all the time in the world. The ground beneath their feet still shook as the Waste circled the facility outside the fence line, looking for a way past the iron wall that shielded them.

"We don't have time to talk about a better idea, just go!"

Coulson pushed Ventura toward the ghost, causing the agent to swear and draw his jacket over his head. To his credit, he didn't even pause, he just ran through the crowd of approaching ghosts and headed for the facility doors, striking a pair of the broken ghosts with his iron baton as he went to thin their numbers.

"Be ready, and be fast," Coulson yelled at Shane over the sound of the rumbling and the moans from the shambling, partially glowing ghosts.

The group had fallen for Ventura's distraction, turning and huddling together to follow him, attracted by the movement more than anything. Only the Burner seemed intelligent enough to realize something was happening, but he was now torn between going after Shane and Coulson or pursuing Ventura to the melted doors.

"I'm ready," Shane said.

He had no clue what Coulson had planned, but the ghost was right. They had no time to plan anything else.

Coulson left his side and walked into the crowd, following the path Ventura had taken. Instead of heading toward the facility door, he approached the Burner. Shane watched, his head turned away and his hand up to protect his eyes, to see what he could through his peripheral vision.

Ventura screamed and stumbled near the door as a blast of burning light scorched the back of his leg and burned through his pants. Shane smelled the burned meat.

Coulson put his hands on the Burner's head, and the light began to dim. They struggled together, and the light from all the nearby ghosts began to dim as well.

Shane joined the crowd, crushing the head of the nearest broken ghost as quickly as he could.

The Burner held Coulson's wrists, and the light flared brighter. Bright and then dark, the Burner's power pulsed as Coulson fought it. The ghosts around them had mostly given up on Ventura and focused their efforts on Coulson. They pulled at him with twisted and broken hands. Some of them strobed with white light, others just looked burned and rotten. They pulled at his arms, back, and face.

Had Coulson been alive, the ghosts would have been tearing the skin from his bones. He held fast, practically dancing with the Burner, struggling against it every time its power flared as though hitting a dimmer switch.

Shane moved from one broken ghost to the next, dragging them to the ground as quickly as he could, and snapping their necks or crushing their faces, putting his hands on their skulls, and using all the force he could muster to crush them quickly.

Each blow knocked him back like someone beating him with a bat. With no rest time between, he found himself gasping for air. His chest was on fire, and his head was swimming. He had destroyed five of the broken things, but there were still so many more swarming on Coulson.

The Burner raged and flared again. Shane watched a piece of Coulson's overcoat burn away, the ghostly fabric igniting and then flaking off. He was losing the battle and unable to keep hold of himself.

Another of the broken spirits strobed from deep within its chest and fell on Ventura. The agent screamed as the heat melted a hole through his jacket and burned his back from shoulder to shoulder.

Coulson's teeth were gritted, and he plunged his thumbs into the Burner's eyes. Shane rushed toward him, avoiding the other broken spirits and intent on getting his hands on the Burner when it blazed brighter than ever.

The light was blinding, painfully so, and Shane stumbled, falling to the ground, and covering his eyes as pain washed over him. It felt like a blast of fire hit him and continued to burn.

"Cover yourself," Coulson screamed as the light grew brighter. "This one's going to be ugly."

CHAPTER 24
ACE IN THE HOLE

Thomas Coulson had always fancied himself a hero. He knew it was arrogant and, even in his head, he rationalized that he didn't want that. He imagined himself saving others from danger, and how gracious and thankful they'd be. And, of course, he'd be humble—but not too humble—in accepting their praise. He would do what no one else could do, and make the world better, and people would love him for it.

It never worked that way. When he gained a full understanding of his power and what he could do with it, he quickly lost any illusions of being a hero. People didn't want a world of good guys and bad guys. They didn't dream of fawning over a man in a white hat. They were selfish and self-involved. They just cared about themselves. They all wanted to be the hero of their story, and everyone else was a villain, a roadblock, or a pain in the ass.

He realized one day that he was no different.

It took a long time for Coulson to accept that people weren't monsters. They weren't selfish, hateful, or inconsiderate. They were normal. Because everyone existed in their own head, everyone had only their thoughts, ideas, and impressions to guide them. None of them knew what anyone else was thinking. Except for Coulson, of course.

Being in other people's heads, seeing what people thought and felt, was a nightmare at first. Especially thoughts that rose on a whim, untampered, and instinctual. The number of people who reacted with anger or hate at the slightest provocation had taken its toll on him. It jaded him, and more than anything, it made him sad.

In time, he grew more tempered in response to the lack of it in others. He realized a person's first instinct was not an indictment of their character. Thoughts came unbidden, and it was the person's nature that decided what happened next.

He needed patience to see that. He needed time to let thoughts develop into ideas and into actions. But it was hard. Before he could fully control his power, before he could shield his mind from the minds of others, those flashes of instinct were the ones that broke through his defenses the most. Pure emotion, usually negative and always powerful. It had made him hate people for a long time.

It took years to build walls. It took Jillian's patience, kindness, and perspective to make him realize that even he was subject to those thoughts, and none of it made him a bad person, so it shouldn't make others bad in his eyes. Most importantly, she made him realize that he could still be a hero even if no one asked him to. Because there were still good people who deserved good things, even if their minds ran dark now and then.

Shane Ryan was a good man. He had more darkness in his soul than many, but Coulson knew he had balanced it well. He had paid a penance for his misdeeds. He did it almost every day, even if he never acknowledged it. Sometimes, that meant embracing the darkness instead of resisting it. He reminded Coulson of himself that way.

When Coulson died, when he sacrificed himself to stop what he was certain was going to be the end of the world, he mostly failed. But he thought it was the right thing to do. And, in the end, what he had predicted had mostly worked out. It was just another person's story, not his. He was not the hero.

Thomas Coulson would not be the hero today, either. His thumbs were buried in the foamy, gelatinous brains of a Burner, and he knew as that strange energy buffeted against his body and tore at the very substance of who he was that this was not his story, either. He should have known better than to call in Shane Ryan, but he wouldn't have gotten the job done without him.

Ventura was down and in pain; Coulson could feel it radiating off him so intensely that he felt the burn on his own back. He would die if he was attacked again. Ryan was blinded, and the burn was already washing over him. They had seconds to spare if that.

"Cover yourself," Coulson screamed as the Burner forced out another wave of energy. It tore at his clothing and the body he had constructed for himself, bound together with the energy of his mind. "This one's going to be ugly."

Since his death, most of Coulson's energy went into maintaining who and what he was. It had been a pleasant distraction. It muted the world and made it so that he could only see into a mind if he tried. He was living almost like everyone else for the first time, and all it took was death to make it happen. It was a surprise, but he was thankful for it.

The Burners, the Burnt Souls, and everything in the desert had tested the strength he had. He had nothing left in the tank.

There was one thing Coulson had left to do, one thing up his sleeve that he always knew was an option but had never tried. He could let go of himself.

Maintaining a body, being an unbound spirit that could walk among the living and talk to them, eat with them, even touch them, was the greatest display of his power, and no one even realized it was happening. But he still had the option to let it go.

As much as he wanted to be thought of as a hero, Thomas Coulson also never wanted to admit that he was afraid. He hadn't even been afraid when his mortal body was torn away from him because he knew what he was doing. He knew in his soul that he was making the right move. But he no longer had that certainty.

The one thing Coulson feared more than anything in the world was not knowing what happened next. Because he had never not known something. When you could read the minds of everyone in the room in a matter of seconds, when you could learn anything there was to know just by thinking about it, it was impossible to not know things.

Until now.

The Burner was white fire in his grip. The world had been swallowed by the great, white nothingness. It pulled at his fake flesh and chewed through the body he had given himself. There were no ghosts, no facility, and no Shane Ryan or Xander Ventura. There was just Thomas Coulson. And he was about to be destroyed, anyway. So, what was he holding on to? What was the point?

There was no time to waste. If he waited, he'd give in to fear and die again anyway. Ryan would die, Ventura would die, and they would have proved nothing. Jillian would never see him again, and she wouldn't even have the satisfaction of knowing his end had a purpose. That was a betrayal, and he would not have it.

Coulson let himself go. The shoes, the rumpled pants, the pale overcoat, and the pack of cigarettes stashed in the breast pocket all faded away like mist. His flesh joined them. Skin so precisely crafted to make him look the way he had when he was alive. The scar on his left thumb, the fine hairs on his wrist and forearm, and the holes in his ears where he'd had them pierced as a teen even though he hadn't worn an earring in decades. Every bit of who he was burst apart like a dream upon waking.

The swell of energy was overwhelming. He felt it from his head to his feet and laughed without making a sound, realizing he had neither a head nor feet. He had no lungs, no mouth, and no face for the laughter to come from. It didn't stop him from doing it, though.

The last thing he would do was worry about rules like that.

The light from the Burner seared through Shane's jacket. He smelled it just as intensely as he felt his flesh starting to burn. He could no longer see Ventura, or even Coulson and the Burner in front of him. When he looked under the edges of the jacket, he saw white and nothing more. But Coulson had told him to duck for cover, so he had.

As quickly as it had ignited, the light from the Burner was vanquished. Even under the jacket, it took a moment for Shane's eyes to adjust to the dark. A blast of wind tore his jacket from his hands, and he was exposed to the night once again. The sound of Coulson laughing echoed through his head like it had come from inside of his mind instead of out in the world. Just a long, deep peel of laughter, and then it faded like the light.

The ground stopped shaking, an abrupt end to the rumbling path of the Waste beneath the sands and its incessant burrowing. Something had happened to stun it to silence.

Everything glowed purple as Shane blinked his eyes to see what was happening. Through bleary vision, he watched as the Burner crumbled to pieces. Coulson was no longer in front of it and no longer holding on to its head. In fact, Shane couldn't see him anywhere.

The other broken spirits had stopped their attack. The ones close to Ventura, and the ones that had ganged up on Coulson flaked apart like ashes being dumped on the ground. Only the pieces faded away and nothing remained of any of them.

Shane kept blinking to make the afterimage of the blinding light go away. It was hard to focus on anything as his vision felt like it was switching between an all-encompassing purple, blinding light, and pure darkness. He only haphazardly caught glimpses of shapes. He saw Ventura's body on the ground, the concrete walls of the facility, and some of the fence posts.

He crawled on his hands and knees, too unstable with his poor vision to risk walking over to Ventura.

"You alive?" He grabbed the other man's arm.

"Yeah." Ventura's reply was more of a gasp than a well-formed word. He shifted his weight, pushing up from the ground awkwardly. Shane could smell the burn on his back. It would need to be bandaged soon to avoid infection, and he'd have a serious scar for the rest of his life.

"What happened?" Ventura asked.

"I don't know. They're gone. All of them," he said.

"Coulson?"

"Gone," Shane said again.

Shane knew the burst of wind that had torn the jacket from his grip and stopped the Waste had to have been Coulson. He had done something, some last-ditch effort. He took the spirits with him and saved their lives. But whatever was in the facility was still there. Whoever or whatever was working below the ground had not been vanquished.

"Did he kill the thing in the ground? The Waste?" Ventura asked.

He sat up and cursed, the burned flesh on his back pulling. The edges of his shirt and jacket had fused into the burn, with the fabric and flesh melting together. When he moved, it tore them free, opening sores that bled freely.

"I don't know. I don't think so," Shane said. The rumbling had stopped a moment after whatever Coulson had done, like it had disturbed but not destroyed the thing in the ground.

Shane had not seen the hunchback ghost before Coulson attacked the Burner. It had not joined the fight. It had probably fled back to the facility.

"Wait here," Shane said. "I'm going to find your hunchback buddy. I think it's time to shut down the PULSE lab and get the hell out of this desert."

Ventura groaned and shook his head, bracing himself before getting his legs under himself and getting to his feet.

"Can't expect me to come all this way and wait outside. I was bait; I earned this," he said. "Let's just go kill whatever's down there."

CHAPTER 25

PHASE THREE

Shane helped Ventura to his feet. The FBI agent looked around them. The desert seemed undisturbed like they had just arrived, and nothing had been waiting for them. There was no sign of anything they had just endured. Even the chasm dug by the Waste beyond the fence had filled in and smoothed out.

Though Ventura's back was the biggest concern, another burn across the rear of his calf had hobbled him. He could walk but he was limping, and the longer he did so, the more likely it was that the wound would get worse. They needed to leave soon.

If Ventura was not going to mention it, neither was Shane. They walked together across the front of the facility toward the melted, steel doors.

The progress would be slow, but Coulson had destroyed everything that was waiting out front. If any guards were still within the facility, their numbers would be severely limited. Shane suspected that if they were resorting to using the broken ghosts, they had nothing left at their disposal. The other Burners and Burnt Souls must still be out in the desert somewhere or swallowed up by the Waste.

"You are very impressive," a voice with a faint Russian accent said as they approached the door.

The hunchback ghost was waiting inside. He approached them, barring their path, and stopped between the two heaps of melted metal. "I did not think to ever see living men so resilient."

"That warms my heart," Shane said. "Is it just you left in here? Just you down there making these things?"

The Russian laughed.

"Making things? Why did you even come to this place? What were you hoping to accomplish? Are you a cowboy? John Wayne come to save the day?"

"John Wayne never slapped the taste out of a hunchback's mouth, so no," Shane said.

The ghost's expression soured, but he did not take the bait. Instead, he offered an awkward shrug.

"You have poor timing no matter what, and you have caused too much trouble. You think you are, what, stopping suffering? These labs have been closed for decades. Perhaps if you came in the seventies, hmm? You could crusade across the desert and save the poor victims, the poor volunteers who chose to be here. Who chose to do this thing. Steal away their autonomy because you know best, hmm?"

"You made monsters out here," Ventura said.

"We made soldiers to kill a monster. And you, look what you did! You fed it. You made it stronger. Phase Two soldiers together could have destroyed it, but you ruined it all. It's free and unchallenged because of you."

"What is?" Shane asked. "What did you do?"

The Russian scoffed, waving a hand dismissively at Shane and turning his back on him as if to leave. He walked two steps before turning back.

"You American cowboys, you heroes, you never look past your noses, hmm? Never stop to ask why something is happening, only how you can involve yourself. And look now. Look what you have done."

"What is the Waste?" Shane asked.

The Russian's sour expression twisted into a grim smile.

"You heard this name, hmm? The Waste. They call it that out there."

The ghost pointed to the desert, to nowhere in particular.

"The ghosts in the mine said it," Shane said, resisting the urge to break the Russian's arms off. He knew more about what was happening, Shane just needed to keep him talking.

"Those were stragglers. Drifters, you call them? Your government told them to stay away, stay out of here for the tests, but you people do not listen. You think you know best, and look what happens. They take cover in the old mines as if radiation would not find them there. They died there, forgotten long ago. Just like you, they should have minded their business."

"The Waste," Shane said again.

"The Waste," the Russian repeated mockingly. "Such a crass name. Your nicknames for everything."

"Then what is it called?"

"It doesn't have a name. It is just Project Five. That's what the scientists called it in the lab when they made it. Project Five. There was never supposed to be such a thing, hmm? It was an accident. A mistake."

"But what is it? How do we stop it?" Shane asked.

The Russian laughed again.

"You don't listen. Phase Two was meant to destroy it. This focused energy tears it apart. It destroys even then dead. It would have destroyed Project Five, but then you came here and released them all. You released Project Five. You ruined it all!"

"We didn't let that thing out," Ventura said. "We came here looking for whatever was destroying the spirits in Doomtown."

"Bah!" the Russian said. "Men like you. Digging up the dead and taking them away. It was all sealed away, you know? For years and years, until the men came. You say they were not with you? Who cares now. Damage is done."

The Russian spit to emphasize his point. He must have been talking about Bennet Ross and those working for him. The ones who had come to dig up the radioactive haunted items. They tripped something like when Shane and the others let the Burners loose at the bunkers. Ross' team had released the Waste, or Project Five, and it began roaming the desert and feasting on the other spirits.

"Where was it before?" Shane said. "If someone released it, then you had it contained. Is there a cell for it, a lead room somewhere? We can lure it back there and trap it again."

The Russian chuckled.

"What brilliant ideas you have. You are so wise. As if I have not been digging toward that prison for weeks now. Weeks! I broke through just yesterday, you know. I found what was left of it. It's melted to slag now. It's nothing!"

"How?" Ventura asked.

"The Phase One failures melted it. They didn't know any better when you released them. You or the men before you. They freed them from their bunker, and they had no control. They burned the prison to the ground, turned it to liquid, and Project Five freed itself. So, the only plan left was to destroy it because it cannot be contained again. It cannot be contained!"

"We can help you," Shane said.

He didn't know what could be done against the Waste. He wasn't even sure he knew what it was, but there had to be a way to get it under control. There were still lead rooms in the bunkers, places where the labs had held the Burners during their experiments. No matter how strong the ghost was, if it was trapped in a lead room, it would not be able to free itself. Then they could bury the lab, and seal it in concrete or lead or whatever it took to make sure no one ever accessed it again.

"You can help me?" The Russian's voice was light and disbelieving. "You have the miracle solution in your pocket?"

"If you want this thing stopped, you can't afford to not accept our help," Ventura said. "We never came here to cause trouble; we came here to fix it."

The Russian ghost laughed again, covering his face in his hands.

"Your ego, my God. Your arrogance. What help can you give now?

They are all gone. Phase One. Phase Two. They are all gone. Do you know what this means? Nothing can stop it now. It can travel farther and farther away. It consumes and grows. It has no boundaries. You know boundaries? The non-biological entity limitations? None! It goes anywhere and does anything. It can eat the whole world now if it wants. Thanks to you."

"If you had told us—" Ventura began.

"Then what, hero?" The Russian cut him off. "You ride your white horse into the sunset? You vanquish the monster? No one asked you to come here! All this trouble, the death of your friend, everything is on your head! Blood is on your hands!"

He shouted the last words, his face twisting in frustration and anger.

Before Shane could say anything, the earth began to shake again. The feeling was different this time. The tremors felt stronger and more striking, and the sand shifted more severely.

The Russian ghost took a hesitant step back, staring down at the ground.

"No! No, you fools! Look what you've done. It's stronger. Smarter now! It went below the wall. It's inside the wall!"

He turned sharply, running back into the facility with surprising speed for one so awkwardly shaped.

"Sergeant Dylan!" the ghost shouted. "Sergeant Dylan!"

The ground cracked, and the concrete wall to the left of the melted steel doors began to crumble. The Waste was below them but tunneling up. Not to the surface of the desert. It was tunneling into the lab.

"Can you make it?" Shane asked.

"Right behind you. Don't wait for me," Ventura said.

Shane nodded and left the agent behind, running into the facility after the Russian ghost.

Past the melted doors, the floor was steel grates. Those near the door had been melted, but new plates had been welded over them at some point.

The first floor was simply a large freight elevator, something for military vehicles or at least large containers. Maybe both. Shane had no idea where the controls were and wouldn't have trusted the ancient piece of machinery even if he did. Next to it was a set of emergency stairs, and he followed them down.

There was nothing to see as Shane took a flight, hit a landing, and then descended a second flight. Red emergency lights illuminated the space, but the walls and floors were blank. No signage or indication of who ran the place or what emergency procedures they had in place.

He reached the next-floor door, which was torn from its hinges. Trash was strewn about in the hallways, and broken windows showed laboratory space. Nothing moved that he saw even after venturing several paces.

The place had been trashed long ago. Portions of the walls and floors were melted away, through solid rock and steel, and it was clear that Burners had been there, or at least the malfunctioning ones that Coulson had vaporized. The Russian must have set them all free. There was nothing now.

Shane descended two more levels of stairs. The walls were lined in lead, but Shane saw places where it had melted through. The problem with binding a ghost in lead rather than its haunted item was very apparent when the ghost could melt metal. Lead melted at a very low temperature. Their attempts to seal the room had failed.

The entire floor looked like it had been holding cells at one point. Nothing but plain, lead-lined rooms and booths. Everything was empty, and much of it was destroyed. The Russian ghost was not there.

Shane descended to another level to the basement of the facility and the last possible door. It, too, had been ripped from its hinges.

The ground shook like an earthquake now and continued to rumble, but the facility was holding strong. The interior walls were not falling apart: The support beams were doing their jobs. The frame, if nothing else, had been built to withstand serious damage.

No red lights were on in the base level, and there was nothing to see in the darkness beyond the door. Shane could not hear the Russian ghost any longer or see any signs that suggested he had gone that way, but there was nowhere else for him to go.

"Are you in here?" Shane yelled into the darkness. The rumbling echoed through what sounded like a large space, and his voice was swallowed by it.

"Yes," a voice replied. It was not Russian. The accent was Texan, but old. It reminded Shane of a tired cowboy from a movie. Maybe that was where the Russian's obsession with them came from.

"Who are you?" Shane asked. He could not see the source of the voice or even judge where it had come from in the dark.

"You can call me Dylan," the voice answered casually. A light appeared in the dark like the sun had dropped from the sky. It was bright but gave off no heat, and Shane could still see through it even if he needed to raise his hand to his eyes. It was painful but tempered.

The source of the light was a man. He was older, he matched his voice, and his face looked grizzled and weather-beaten. His chest and torso were gone, replaced with a pulsing sphere of energy that thrummed like a heartbeat. The rest of his body, his arms and legs, looked glossy and fake. They were arranged around the central sphere in the proper place, but it didn't look to Shane like they were attached well. It looked like the ghost was birthing a small star in the center of his body.

"They used to call me Phase Three around here."

CHAPTER 26

GROUND ZERO

Dylan had illuminated a massive underground chamber. Shane saw a control panel far behind him, a bank of ancient computers, and monitors set against the wall. Closer was a tunnel, much smaller than the ones dug by the Waste but still made by hand from the looks of it. Rubble from the tunnel was strewn about the room.

"He is coming, Sergeant Dylan," the Russian ghost said, passing through the room toward the computers at the far end.

"I know, Yuri," the glowing ghost replied, keeping his eyes on Shane. "You shouldn't be here."

"Looks to me like a lot of things shouldn't be here," Shane said.

The glowing ghost made a face that was neither a smile nor a smirk but seemed otherwise uninterested in Shane's opinion.

"Sergeant Dylan is our only hope now," Yuri said from the far side of the room. "You are in his way. He is the only successful Phase Three soldier. More powerful than anything before. More than you or your mysterious friend, hmm?"

"Then why haven't you stopped it yet?"

"Oh, such a critical mind," Yuri said sarcastically, checking monitors as the rumbling increased. "Why don't the police just stop all crime? Why doesn't your President outlaw poverty and doctors cure all diseases? Maybe you should run the world Your ideas are so cutting-edge."

"Yuri…" Dylan said softly.

"He will get us all killed," the Russian said harshly.

"We're already dead," Dylan replied.

"He will get the world killed. He doesn't know anything. He doesn't know Project Five. He doesn't know danger. He's a stupid, bald man who punches ghosts like a monkey."

"Yuri has been working on this for many years," the other ghost explained. "He literally gave his life to this project."

"Seems like you did, too," Shane said.

"As a volunteer."

"And you can destroy the Waste?"

"The Waste," the ghost mused. "I was made to destroy anything. Everything."

"What is it? Was it made here like you? Like the Burners?"

In the background, Yuri finished making his adjustments on the control panel and scoffed, shuffling away from it.

"He wants explanations now. As if he has standing," the Russian said.

"You'd be curious as well, Yuri," Dylan said.

"I would not have come here at all," Yuri countered. "I am not such a fool."

"Project Five was an accident, nothing more. Instead of sealing it away when it happened, they chose to play with it until they could no longer control it. And then someone let it out. That's all there is to know," Dylan explained.

"From what I saw, there's a lot more to know," Shane countered. The ghost shrugged.

Beneath them, the rumbling had increased again, and Yuri shook his head.

"Three feet of iron." The ghost stomped his foot. "And still it comes."

"How?" Shane asked.

"It is like a cyclone," Yuri said. "Digging, clawing, and spinning. Iron causes a reaction to return the spirit to its source, but Project Five *is* the source! It is back and forth. Dig, reaction, dig, reaction. So many hands, and so many spirits. It cannot be stopped. One leaves, another replaces it, again and again and again. It will break through, and then we will see."

Yuri looked at Dylan, who turned his head, not enough to see the ghost but enough to acknowledge his words. The burning ghost smiled gently and nodded.

"We will see," he agreed.

"You've never fought it. You don't know if you'll defeat it," Shane said.

"Of course not. Neither of us has ever been free from here before. Neither of us was supposed to be freed."

"You volunteered to be a prisoner," Shane said.

"I volunteered to save my country. To do my duty," Dylan countered sharply. "From any enemy."

"But they never built you for this, did they? You were supposed to fight, what, the Russians?" Shane nodded at Yuri.

"Any enemy," Dylan repeated.

"Even one that has never been tested. If you fail, what's left?"

"Thanks to you? Nothing," Yuri said sourly. "If Project Five is too powerful, there is no hope."

"Then let me help you," Shane said. "I didn't release that thing, but I don't want it escaping this desert any more than you do."

"And how would you help?" Dylan was bemused by Shane's offer.

"He is a Non-Standard," Yuri said.

"A Delta?" Dylan was suddenly curious.

"No. The one he left outside is a Delta. He is an Alpha. There was a third, but I do not know what he was. Dead now, so it doesn't matter," Yuri explained.

"An Alpha?" Dylan said. He reached out a hand and Shane reacted swiftly, catching the ghost by the wrist. His skin felt cool but much softer than any spirit he had encountered. It was almost gelatinous.

Dylan smiled for the first time, looking at Shane's hand on his wrist.

"I never met a real Alpha," he said.

"I'm sure that's fascinating," Shane said, "but I don't think we have time for your code words and special memories."

"We don't have time for anything," Dylan said. "Including you."

The ghost's chest began to thrum, and the light output increased dramatically. The almost normal human face collapsed, as did the body. Bone and muscle seemed to cave in all over Dylan, replaced by an amorphous mass of sloppy, pulsating tissue. What was left no longer resembled a human but a tumorous flesh mass surrounding a core of pure light that grew brighter by the second.

"I can help you," Shane repeated.

The thing that Dylan had become twisted and grew larger. Yuri chuckled behind it.

"You think we are fools? You destroyed Phase Two. You will die here, and your handlers will learn that even an Alpha has no place here," Yuri shouted.

A column of throbbing, seeping flesh reached for Shane from around the glowing center mass of Dylan's body. He caught it and screamed. Though there was no glow, the flesh burned as if it were on fire.

Shane pulled away quickly and cradled his hand to his chest as he stepped back. The contact was quick, but the burn was severe, possibly second-degree in some places where he had applied the most pressure. His skin was already blistering.

He stepped away as Dylan grasped at him with a fleshy appendage like a tentacle. He could not discern what might have qualified as the spirit's head and was not sure how he would lay hands on it to destroy it even if he did see it.

The ground shook, and pieces of the building finally began to show wear from the onslaught of the Waste below them, ceaselessly burrowing through the iron shield that had been set up to protect the lab. A slab of stone from inside Yuri's tunnel fell, caving in the entrance and taking a wall with it.

Something in the computer control panel shorted out, and a red light began to flash as the klaxon alarm went off again. Yuri left to fix it as Dylan stayed focused on Shane.

The burning ghost forced him back toward the stairwell, and Yuri began yelling from back in the room.

"He's almost through the shield. We have to prepare!"

Two tentacles of pulsing, oozing flesh reached out for Shane. He raised his hands, ready to defend himself when something on the steps behind him clanged loudly, a repeated banging that sounded over the alarm and the quaking of the structure.

Ventura stood at the top of the last flight of stairs, looking down at Shane and Dylan. He pounded the iron baton on the stair railing until the ghost stopped his approach. He had no face and no eyes, but Ventura had gotten his attention.

"This is not on our side?" Ventura yelled down.

"Not on our side," Shane confirmed.

Ventura threw the iron baton. The weapon spun end over end and thumped against the widest expanse of oozing, tumorous flesh. Dylan was gone in a blink, and the baton hit the ground.

Ventura awkwardly made his way down the rest of the steps, steadying himself on the railing until he reached Shane.

"What the hell—"

"Phase Three," Shane said. "The Waste is breaking in here any minute, iron doesn't stop it, and it can't be contained in lead anymore. You ready?"

"Jesus," the agent said. That was the best Shane could have hoped for.

"You are a fool!" Yuri came for Shane in the red light of the incessant alarm. "You will destroy everything!"

He moved swiftly, hobbling side to side before lunging at Shane in the doorway. His appearance was deceptive, and his body was quick and far more agile than it appeared. He swarmed Shane, clawing and kicking and even biting as he took him to the ground.

They rolled together as the building shook, and a chunk of the ceiling caved in, nearly collapsing on Ventura, who was forced back into the stairwell.

Shane struggled with Yuri, his burned hand making the fight harder than it should have been. The hunchback sunk his teeth into Shane's left shoulder, causing Shane to bite off a scream. It felt like chisels made of ice were digging into the meat as the ghost tried to bite off a piece.

With his right hand, Shane reached over Yuri's body and grasped at the exposed wound on the ghost's back. His fingers closed over the rigid, raised segment of spine and he grabbed hold, wrenching back with all his strength.

Yuri's mouth released as he cried out in surprise, trying to reach his back but failing due to the intrusive hump of flesh in his way.

The ghost stared panic-stricken into Shane's eyes as his spine broke and pulled up. Shane yanked as hard as he could, dislodging the ghost's spinal column from his back and pulling it loose. It peeled out of Yuri's back like a loose thread from a sweater until it reached the base of the ghost's skull. Then, with one final, powerful pull, Shane yanked the ghost's head from his body.

Shane's arm jerked as the tension released. Yuri's head, attached to his spine, sailed wide and to the right before crunching on the facility floor. It exploded, along with the rest of his body, pushing the air from Shane's lungs with the force of the blast.

The alarm wailed, and the building quaked as Shane gasped for air. The floor in the center of the room cracked and bulged upward before sinking down again. Dark hands grasped at the pieces in the red light, and Shane struggled to his feet.

Just as Shane righted himself, a scream pierced through the cacophony. It screeched louder than the alarm, and Shane covered his ears.

The red light was overwhelmed by pure white. Dylan had returned, and the smoldering ball of energy in his chest blazed like the sun. The Waste roared in a dozen voices at the same time, retreating and letting the floor cave into the hole it had burrowed, but Dylan pushed forward.

Shane could smell his flesh burning as he collapsed, scrambling for the stairwell and a potential escape. Dylan's enraged wail chased him, and the light seared his hands when he reached out, inches from the stairwell door, forcing him to pull in as he curled into a ball to avoid the blazing power the ghost emitted.

"Move your ass," a voice said in his ear.

A cold hand grabbed Shane by the collar and yanked him out of the room and into the stairwell. The smell of Coulson's cigarette blew in his face stronger than the faint meaty smell of his flesh.

"Be quick this time," Coulson said, though Shane could not see him.

He pulled the jacket from his head and saw Ventura on the ground a few feet away, blocking his face but peering over the edge looking as confused as Shane felt.

The blinding light in the doorway flickered and then dimmed. Shane was on his feet as quickly as he could. He had no idea where Coulson had come from, or how, but it didn't matter.

Shane raced into the room, jumping over a crack in the floor caused by the Waste and toward Dylan, who stood at the precipice of the hole, struggling in Coulson's grasp.

Coulson was forcing the light down, with the pulsing in Dylan's chest struggling to even reach the brightness of a normal lightbulb. Shane didn't hesitate, he just plunged his hands into the throbbing mass of flesh and began tearing.

There was no heat left in the ghost's body. The oozy, gelatinous quality of the flesh made it weak and pliable. He tore pieces off by the handful as Coulson held it steady. Slabs of it fell apart under Shane's onslaught as he looked for something to focus his efforts on. If Dylan had a head, or a brain, anywhere in the mass of tissue he had become, Shane was intent on destroying it.

Shane's hand fell on something warm and solid. He pulled at it, sinking his nails into it and using all his might to separate it from the whole. The pulsing sphere of energy in Dylan's core tore away from the flesh sheath that held it.

The ghost screamed from a mouth it didn't have. Shane yanked the glowing core free and tossed it toward the hole in the floor. It burst before it fell, releasing a powerful blast of energy that knocked Shane across the room.

The alarm was still sounding, and the red light was still flashing. Shane was on his back, staring at the ceiling as it strobed from red to black. His back hurt, so did his legs and hands. It was still a struggle to breathe, but it was getting better.

Coulson appeared above him, looking down into his face. The cigarette dangled from his lips, looking precariously close to falling on him.

"You still alive?" he asked.

"Are you?" Shane asked.

Though it was still Coulson, something was different about him now. For the first time since they had met, he looked like a ghost. There was no illusion and no sense that he was a real man like before. He was just a spirit.

"Haven't been for a long while now," Coulson answered.

Shane sat up. The building was still. The deafening alarm had not ceased, but the shaking had ended. The Waste had left, fearful of Dylan, and the facility was empty.

"Firefly scared off the monster," Coulson said as Shane got to his feet. "It's still down there somewhere."

"He said he was the only thing that could defeat it," Shane said.

Coulson shrugged, leaning over the edge, and looking down at the hole.

"Yeah. We might have just screwed up everything," he agreed.

"We should get out of here in case anyone's monitoring that alarm,"

Ventura said from the doorway. "Hey, Coulson."

"Ventura," Coulson said.

They left the room together, with Shane helping Ventura up the steps until they reached the top. Outside, the desert sky was just beginning to lighten as the sun rose. The rumbling of the Waste was long gone. The desert was as still and silent as ever, except for a series of distant lights growing closer from the east.

"What is that?" Ventura asked.

"Humvees," Coulson answered. "Looks military."

Shane was not in any condition or mood to run, nor was Ventura. He sat next to the concrete wall of the lab facility and pulled out a cigarette. The first of the Humvees arrived just as he exhaled the first puff of smoke.

A trio of military police exited the first vehicle, their weapons drawn and aimed at Ventura and Shane. Coulson was nowhere to be seen.

"On your stomach," one of the armed men yelled. More armed soldiers poured from the second vehicle, as did a man in combat fatigues with no discernible rank displayed anywhere on his uniform. A patch on his chest read "Hawke."

"Agent Xander Ventura and Mr. Shane Ryan," Hawke said. "What a pleasure to meet you."

One of the armed men slipped a black bag over Shane's head as he was forced to the ground. Handcuffs locked over his wrists, and he was half-carried to one of the vehicles.

"What the hell is going on? Who are you?" Ventura demanded.

Shane said nothing. The men were not going to answer questions now, but they'd find out what they needed to know soon enough.

EPILOGUE

The refrigerator in the trailer made an ominous humming sound even with the door closed. Dezzy had hoped that if he made quick trips in and out, it would somehow fix itself and last longer. To that end, he opened it quickly, pulled out some leftover chicken and two cans of Pepsi Lime, and then slammed the door closed.

It was hard to resist the urge to bring Doc out to talk. Dezzy was a social creature by nature. He had spent far too many years dead and hadn't had a lot of opportunities to just hang out and trade small talk with people. And whenever he saw people, they were typically not in the mood for chitchat. Being dead did not have a lot of upsides.

Now that he was alive again, he was happy to experience everything the world had to offer, including all the things he never knew existed when he was alive before. Plus things that really didn't exist back then, like Pepsi Lime and XBox.

His second chance at life had taken him to unusual places where he met unusual people, both living and dead. As far as he could tell, it was just fate's hand guiding him, and he was more than willing to let it. He would go where he needed to go and be where he needed to be when the universe made it happen.

"So far so good," he said to himself to confirm it. So, what if he had to spend time alone in a trailer in the desert? Something was going to happen soon.

He left the trailer and sat in one of the folding lawn chairs out front with a big beach umbrella stuck in the sand next to him to extend the reach of the trailer's awning and provide shade.

There was no real relief from the heat in the shade. But he wasn't going to get a sunburn, even though his dusky skin rarely burned.

He stared out at the desert and the town of Benton and made short work of a fried chicken drumstick. Normally, he would have been responsible with his trash and thrown it away, but a coyote had been coming by the trailer, and he'd taken to feeding it the chicken bones. He tossed the meatless drumstick as far as he could into the sand and then opened a Pepsi with greasy fingers, struggling to lift the pull tab.

It had been some time since he'd seen Coulson. Part of him thought he should worry about that, but a bigger part knew that Thomas Coulson was probably the most capable being on earth, except for maybe their friend Vincent. Or his Uncle Stanley. Whatever they went hunting in the desert would be no match for them.

Dezzy swallowed a mouthful of Pepsi, savoring the cool, sweet liquid as it contrasted with the leftover hint of saltiness from the chicken he'd just eaten. Everything in the world tasted better since he'd come back from the dead. Sometimes, he thought he should just go from town to town eating everything there was to eat until he'd tasted the entire world. Then, he realized he didn't have the funds for it and was happy to take what he could get.

The sun was close to its apex, and there was no breeze to speak of. There was a small scattering of clouds in the sky, the little, puffy, cotton-looking ones, but just three that he saw. In all those miles of sky, just a few poofs. The day was made to just sit and be hot.

Every so often, he saw light reflecting off a car driving through Benton. The road was not a popular one, and tourists in the area were either looking for Death Valley or Las Vegas. If anyone wanted to see the desolate and forbidden zone where they used to test nukes, they usually did it from the eastern side. You could get close to Area 51 over there. There was nothing on the Benton side.

Dezzy started gnawing on a chicken breast, the breading crunching loudly under his teeth and flaking over his shirt. He muttered his dissatisfaction with losing crumbs and picked the edible pieces off his chest as the ground beneath his feet began to vibrate.

He froze in place with a Pepsi in one hand and chicken in the other, watching as the vibrations ran up through his chair and into his body, shaking the crumbs onto the ground.

"Oh, man," he said softly, getting to his feet.

The trailer windows began to rattle, and some of Doc's stuff fell from the shelves. Dust rose in clouds, and Dezzy stumbled away from the trailer as it shifted and rocked. The shaking became violent, and he fell over as something rolled on the ground beneath the trailer, lifting it, and setting it down again as though the sand had become liquid, and a wave had come crashing through.

Dezzy dropped the chicken and the Pepsi and ran for the town of Benton. The wave of sand was rolling toward it, not particularly high but very wide. Something was beneath the ground, and it was moving quickly.

Coulson and Jillian and Vincent had powers, but Dezzy knew the dead when he felt them. He was still connected to the world beyond, to the place from which the dead were not supposed to return. Whatever had passed him below the sand was dead.

He ran as fast as his feet would carry him across the sand, but the thing in the ground was faster. It was heading for town, for the diner, and the motel at the edge of town. He had to warn the people to leave, even if he couldn't say why.

It was not a great distance between the trailer and the town, but it was far enough. Too far. As Dezzy ran, he watched the motel walls collapse.

The building fell, and the windows of the diner shattered. Dezzy barely heard it, but he saw the fragments burst and catch the light like a thousand stars falling out of the walls.

The closer he got, the louder the rumbling became, and the more certain he was that there were screams mixed in with the cacophony.

Dust rose from the ground at the motel, at the diner, across the road and everywhere else he could see. Benton was not a big town; it was barely a town at all. Not even a hundred people lived there anymore and most, save for a small handful, were concentrated in the same couple of blocks around the diner, the motel, and the gas station.

Light burst from the ground, rising in plumes like fire in a dozen places. The earth beneath the town was falling in, first the motel, and then the diner, and then everything down the road after it. Benton was being sucked below in a chain reaction.

Buildings broke like dry crackers and glass shattered. A great explosion from the gas station rose into the sky, all orange fire and black smoke until it, too, was swallowed and smothered, as if the thing in the earth denied even the power of flame to exist on the surface.

The surrounding sands pulled forward as the earth supporting them gave way. It was like watching the tide come in, with sand suddenly rushing into a chasm and dragging cacti and stones with it.

The thing beneath the earth had tunneled under the highway and pulled everything down on top of itself. Dezzy stopped running and watched as hands rose from the yellow flames and dust clouds. Hands made of hands, arms made of multiple limbs joined together, some kind of nightmare homunculus born from countless others. It was like a giant made of the dead, and it dragged the town of Benton into the earth in seconds.

The quaking reached its crescendo as the last of the buildings in Benton succumbed, crumbled to pieces, and were pulled into the chaos. It ended as quickly as it began. For a moment only, there was silence. Benton was gone, and the desert was as quiet as a grave. But only for a moment.

The rumbling began again, rolling under the earth, away from Dezzy and from what had once been Benton. Whatever it was, it was finished and was on the move again.

Dezzy reached the edge of the town as the earth filled the hole with sand and rubble. There were fragments of the buildings and chunks of wood, glass, and metal, but nothing was even large enough to be identifiable. It was like Benton had been run through a meat grinder.

He wanted to look for survivors, but his gut told him to stay back. Not out of fear that the hole might be unstable or that he'd put himself at risk. It was the same thing that told him the entity beneath the ground was dead. He knew there were no survivors. The dead thing that came for Benton came for its people. It swallowed them and left again.

Dezzy wanted to find Coulson and warn him about the thing beneath the ground, but it was heading in the direction Coulson had gone. If Coulson wasn't already looking for it, it would be looking for him soon enough. But Dezzy's gut told him something else, too. The thing under the ground had something more in mind than Thomas Coulson. And he had the distinct feeling that it was feeding so it could be ready.

⋯⧫⋯

Check out these best-selling series from our talented authors:

GHOST STORIES

RON RIPLEY
BERKLEY STREET SERIES
MOVING IN SERIES
HAUNTED COLLECTION SERIES
DEATH HUNTER SERIES

IAN FORTEY
JIGSAW OF SOULS SERIES
CULT OF THE ENDLESS NIGHT SERIES

SUPERNATURAL SUSPENSE

A. I. NASSER
SLAUGHTER SERIES
SIN SERIES

DAVID LONGHORN
NIGHTMARE SERIES
ASYLUM SERIES

SARA CLANCY
THE BELL WITCH SERIES
BANSHEE SERIES

For a complete list of our new releases and best-selling horror books, visit ScareStreet.com or scan the QR code below!

www.ingramcontent.com/pod-product-compliance
Lightning Source LLC
Chambersburg PA
CBHW050345030726
47503CB00008B/2623